DATE DUE

SEP 1 2 2011			
JAN 0 7 2012			
JAN 3 0 2012			

Demco

BURNING HORSES

A HUNGARIAN LIFE TURNED UPSIDE DOWN

AGATHA HOFF

BURNING HORSES
A HUNGARIAN LIFE TURNED UPSIDE DOWN

AGATHA HOFF

SWEET EARTH FLYING PRESS

DEDICATED TO ÉVA,

WHO HAS GONE HOME TO JÓSKA,

AND TO HER GREAT-GRANDDAUGHTERS,

VANESSA, LITTLE EVA, AND SARAH,

WHO CARRY ON

"WE TWO KEPT HOUSE THE PAST AND I, THE PAST AND I,
I TENDED WHILE IT HOVERED NIGH—LEAVING ME N'ER ALONE"

UNKNOWN ENGLISH POET, 1600

CONTENTS

Preface by Agatha Hoff

Burning Horses is the story of my mother Éva—Jewish by ancestry, but Catholic by upbringing—and our family, whose lives were torn asunder by the Nazi and Soviet occupations of Hungary during World War II.

My mother, although baptized, was not raised as a practicing Catholic, except in a very superficial way. Though she became painfully aware of her Jewish ancestry, she was and remained secular, yet never formally left the Church. Éva's story is not one of conversion, yet alone the emergence of a Zionist.

Mama's life spanned some of the most important events of the twentieth century, mostly experienced in her native Hungary. Like millions of others, she was an individual caught up in historic events beyond her control. I have chosen to tell the story of her life, only marginally placing it in the larger context of world events. She struggled foremost to keep body and soul together for herself and her family.

In the 1970s and 1980s, my mother lived upstairs from my family in San Francisco. On precious, rare occasions, my husband would take care of the children so Mama and I could escape our responsibilities and walk in the Presidio, near our home. I remember late one Memorial Day afternoon, we climbed to the top of the National Cemetery, one of our favorite spots, that afforded a magnificent view. The headstones cast elongated shadows on the grass carpeting the soldiers' graves. Referring to her father, my mother said, ."Apu was here covering the dedication of the bridge in 1937. He missed being in Budapest when you were born. He had a job to do." Another snippet of family lore had come to my attention.

Mama was a wonderful raconteur, so we often included her in social occasions, particularly if we were entertaining guests who had not met one another before. Éva would provide the glue to hold a gathering together by pulling a suitable anecdote from her past to enthrall our friends. On these occasions, she was very selective in what she recounted and avoided subjects most painful to her.

Mama—the repository of our family lore—died in 1992. For months afterwards, hardly a day went by without some family member's having a question for Mama. Now, many years later, my sister Livia and I still frequently say, "Mama would have known."

In the years since my mother's death, I occasionally made notes of some of those anecdotes Éva imparted at odd moments to add to the 100 plus pages she herself had typed. Still, some events in my mother's life went unspoken or unrecorded, perhaps out of fear that she could not hold her emotions in check or that she had to adhere to her generational demand for propriety and decorum.

When I followed my sister into retirement a few years ago, it occurred to me that soon there would be no one who remembered the details of our mother's life. She left few heirlooms, only stories. Thus, the idea for writing *Burning Horses* was born. I began expanding her writings by filling in gaps from my own recollections, including some of those difficult events that she chose not to relate.

My mother never knew how much I saw and heard when I was a child. We each maintained a code of silence around some of the more traumatic experiences. Éva, however, never stopped reminiscing, albeit selectively.

At first I attempted to write Mama's story as a narrator, but I kept hearing her voice and her expressions, almost as if she were trying to tell me what to say. I decided to let Éva tell her own story in the first person. I beg the reader's indulgence about conversations recounted in the book which are of necessity imagined or reconstructed, not an oddity in the fickle world of memory. Though I tried to stay faithful to her writings and her stories, no doubt there are words used in this narrative that she may never have said and which I needed to have her say.

I wish Mama were alive to correct discrepancies and I ask the reader to keep in mind that I have written this book well after the fact and tried to include what I felt was most meaningful. I found that it is a complex matter to write about a life, much of which took place during a very volatile phase of global history. In a way, it put Mama's life at my mercy. Had my sister, or anyone else, written this book, it might have been completely different due to our very different personalities and memories.

It is, therefore, important for me to note that much of this narrative is dependent on twice-remembered accounts, once by my mother, once by me, in the retelling of events that happened many years ago. I can only claim that this story is true insofar as memory allows. Mama's story exemplifies the indomitable human spirit surviving during the volatile first half of the twentieth century.

Acknowledgments

First, thank you to my mother, Éva Badics, without whose storytelling this book could never have been written.

For their help in the preparation of this book, my warmest thanks to my publisher, Sōndra Banfield Dailey; my editor, Maceo Crenshaw Dailey, Jr.; Joe Evanisko of the University of California Extension, without whose help I would have abandoned the project; to the Thursday Writers, Jane Dachtelberg, Jeanne Angier, Rena Bancroft, Inka Benton, Yvonne Cannon, Marie Haas, Jan Lurie, Claire Mack, Ruth Oates, and Carolyn Welshans, who midwifed the manuscript; to my son Joseph DeLappe and his wife Laurie Macfee, whose artistic suggestions and computer skills sped this process along; and forever to my husband, Irwin Hoff, for his patience and encouragement.

Note to the Reader

Agatha Hoff's reconstruction of her mother's life is based on Éva Leopold Badic's writings, the many discussions between both of them, and Agatha's childhood memories. The story is told as if Éva herself were telling it.

Introduction by Éva Leopold Badics

Until I learned of the opening of the hotel at Cservölgy (the Valley of the Oaks) in Hungary, I felt content to let the story of my life fade with the passage of time and to let the scene of my happiest years be slowly overgrown with weeds and wildflowers. The news that the old, stately mansion had been restored and the Camelot of my dreams now catered to German tourists particularly upset me. The worst thing about it is that, with the exception of my daughters, Livia and Aggie, there is no one in the world who cares.

Before World War II, Cservölgy was a beautiful farm of rolling hills and blossoming fruit trees. It is the place we called home.

Livia, Aggie, and I decided not to reclaim the property at the time the Russian troops were withdrawn in 1989. We thought the land surrounding the house would continue to be farmed by the peasants, who for forty years during the Russian occupation had worked it as a collective. Instead, the state sold it to the developer of the hotel.

I know that neither the owners nor the tourists are responsible for the actions of the Nazis. However, the fact that the Germans tore our lives asunder leaves me feeling raw when I think of their descendants cavorting at Cservölgy.

I turned eighty a few months ago, and my recollections of the past are becoming sharper, almost as if a spotlight was being turned on events of long ago. I have tried to block some of the less desirable images with sleeping pills, but in the end, many nights I sit alone in front of my ancient Royal typewriter in my San Francisco apartment and wile away my insomnia by writing.

Perhaps my girls will read this when I'm gone, and remember.

The Rocking Horse

Across the landscape of my dreams, horses gallop and gallop about and I am running, filled with joy, trying to catch one. Just as I reach for the mane of the black stallion to swing myself up onto his glistening back, the horse is enveloped in flames. They leap and dance with fury, and I shield my face from the intense heat, staggering backward to escape the fire. From the crackling inferno, the stallion gallops toward me, his mane blazing.

The dream abruptly shifts, and I am cold, so cold. I find myself crying out for help, thrusting my hands and arms upward from a pool of excrement in which I am drowning. The stench is overwhelming.

I wake, drenched with perspiration, and shake my head to escape the familiar nightmare. The dream arouses so many memories that I know sleep will not come again.

My thoughts drift to a time when I was three years old.

A splendid rocking horse stood in the corner of my nursery. My mother's father, Grandpa Jacobi, had given it to me. The little black stallion seemed to regard a portrait of me on the wall. In the painting, I'm wearing jodhpurs and a velvet riding jacket, my green eyes reflect my joy, and my red hair is flying. I am sitting on his back and holding the reins of my pony, Macaroni.

Four generations of my family had lived in Szekszárd, a small town in southern Hungary, in the early 1800s. Over the next century many Jews, including my parents, who had converted from Judaism as adults, joined the Catholic Church, the Hungarian national religion. Grandpa Jacobi did not convert. Perhaps his massive physical presence, piercing blue eyes, and thick white beard and hair exempted him from having to conform. My mother often related that when I was baptized at the age of one month, Grandpa took pleasure in giving an elaborate toast at the party afterward, ending with "l'chaim." Some thought he was just forgetful, and the Catholics who were present smirked a bit behind his back. I think he threw in the Hebrew on purpose. What finer toast could there be for a baby than "to life"!

Other than this oft-repeated anecdote, neither of my parents ever discussed in my presence anything about our Jewish forebears, nor did we celebrate any Jewish traditions.

Later, when I started school, the five or six Jewish children in my class were excused from attending on Jewish holidays. By long-standing tradition, the rest of us Catholics sneered and made fun of them for wearing yarmulkes (skull caps) and *payess* (sideburns, uncut locks of hair). I was glad I wasn't a Jew. Some made fun of Grandpa for walking around Szekszárd wearing a yarmulke. They made me feel uncomfortable because I loved my grandpa, so I pretended not to notice that he wore one.

"Why does Grandpa go around with a skull cap?" I asked Mother on one such occasion.

"He's a stubborn old man," she replied, dismissing the subject without further explanation.

Later that day, I overheard Mother relate my question to my father.

"What she doesn't know won't hurt her," Apu said. "We're Catholics. That's all she needs to know."

I learned then that Grandpa's being a Jew was a touchy subject, to be left alone. Grandpa kept his opinions to himself, never enlightening me. I blended in with my Catholic peers.

There must have been a strange configuration of stars in the heavens when my parents fell in love, or perhaps the scarcity of Jewish families in Szekszárd had narrowed their choices. Though they had a certain intellectual curiosity in common, my father and mother were as different as fire and ice. Apu was an egalitarian and a forgetful dreamer, full of passion and fun; Mother, a serious scholar, a pragmatist, and an elitist.

A glamorous, life-size oil portrait of my mother at age twenty-two hung above the mantle dominating the living room. She was depicted wearing a beaded, full-length, pink taffeta gown. Her long, auburn hair, combed back in a chignon, showed off her bare shoulders and accented her slim figure. I felt my mother's penetrating brown eyes looking right through me. My father, who stood in the shadows behind her in the painting, towered over her at six-feet-two-inches in height. A small, elegant brass plaque centered at the bottom of the painting identified my parents as "Livia and Lajos Leopold—1904".

Apu often said I was a carbon copy of Mother. I had her oval face, elegant nose, and gently curved lips, but his blond hair and blue eyes combined with her features to give me red hair and green eyes.

Our home stretched across the crest of a hill, visible from most of the town. Each of us, including Apu and Mother, had our own bedroom, and the house was large enough to accommodate a number of guests. A bathtub with running water was so new in those days that my father pretended he didn't know how to turn on the faucets and would have the servants run his bath for him. The servants occupied rooms in the basement. In the living room and the library, the slipcovers, on the large comfortable armchairs, were routinely changed by the servants to match the seasons: flowery chintz in the spring and summer, when freshly cut flowers decorated the tables; an autumn leaf pattern in the fall; and in winter, a warm, rusty velvet, with pillows in a gold tone, to reflect the crackling flames in the stone fireplace. A grand piano stood near the bay window in the living room, and I learned to play at age five.

During my early childhood, my favorite member of the household, perhaps even outranking Apu and Mother, was Borcsa *néni* (a term of affection and respect), our cook. Though as a little girl I thought of her as an old woman, in reality she must have been in her late thirties. Her kind face had a unique feature—that of a single prominent tooth protruding. Her crease-filled face could break into a radiant smile at the slightest compliment of her culinary skills. She had been the family cook all of her adult life, and spent most of her waking hours concocting soufflés, or baking cakes or pastries. I especially loved her chocolate frosting, made with bulk chocolate Mother ordered from America.

Besides Borcsa *néni*, my parents employed a coachman named Karcsi who took care of the horses and the carriage; a maid, Kati; and a footman, Pál. It embarrassed me that I was the only child in Szekszárd with a governess imported from England. She spoke to me only in English, which I was learning to grasp in spite of myself. Over the years, all our governesses were called Mary, whether or not that was their true name.

Among the Hungarian upper crust, Mary seemed to be the generic name used for governesses. Mother loved imports, whether people or things, and had all our clothes tailor-made in London.

Budapest

The Great War

June 28, 1914, when I was almost nine, World War I was triggered by the shooting of Archduke Ferdinand at Sarajevo by a Serb nationalist. Apu, in his job as a newspaper columnist, wrote passionate articles, debating the pros and cons of declaring war on the Serbs in retaliation.

One evening, shortly after the assassination, Mother and I were dining by torchlight on the veranda outside the dining room of our Szekszárd home, and enjoying the coolness of the summer evening. Apu was late getting home from work, so we had started without him. The footman served white asparagus on a silver dish that reflected the flickering candles set on the table. A shower of shooting stars, which I had never witnessed before, made me feel small and insignificant and for some reason sad.

Apu usually announced his arrival home by whistling "Yankee Doodle." I would jump up, run, and give him a hug. On this particular night, though, he appeared without making a sound. I noticed him standing in the shadow of the archway leading to the veranda, observing Mother and me. His unusual behavior prompted me to keep still and pretend I hadn't seen him. He pulled a handkerchief from his pocket and mopped his forehead before stepping forward. It wasn't hot, so I couldn't understand why he was perspiring. He stopped frowning when he realized I was observing him, but did not greet me.

Instead, in a solemn voice, he announced, "We are at war."

Mother gasped, and with a gesture she often used when she was upset, reached up to smooth her hair in place. I noticed that her hand was shaking.

"It's past your bedtime, Éva," she told me. Her face in the distorting torchlight had a purple tinge as she said this, making me feel uneasy.

Again I looked at the night sky: a shooting star crossed the horizon. I wanted to hear what Apu had to say, but no one argued with Mother, so I kissed her and Apu good night and headed into the house without finishing my dinner.

I could hear snatches of my parents' conversation while I lay in bed in my room that overlooked the veranda. As I drifted toward sleep, I heard Apu exclaim, "I'm going to volunteer, first thing tomorrow." A cold feeling arose in the pit of my stomach. Although I strained my ears, I could not hear Mother's reply. I continued to listen as my parents talked softly, long into the night, and slept fitfully, dreaming of Apu riding on a gray horse, his saber drawn.

True to his word, Apu marched off to enlist the next morning at the temporary recruiting station that had been set up hastily at the Szekszárd post office. Men from all over the region were streaming into town to enlist.

At about lunchtime, I spotted Apu coming back up the hill toward our house and ran to meet him.

"They wouldn't take me, Éva," he said, his eyes downcast. "They told me I have flat feet." He kicked a stone toward the gutter, raising a dust cloud. "I'm going to be the laughing stock of Szekszárd—the only man left here with all the women and children."

I found myself torn between being happy that Apu would be staying home and wanting him riding into battle on the gray stallion of my dreams, with his saber glinting in the sunlight. "I'm sorry you won't be going to war, since that's what you wanted, but glad you'll be here with me."

He smiled at me and held my hand the rest of the way home, while I scurried to keep up with his long stride.

By the time Mother returned from shopping later that afternoon, Apu had devised another plan.

"I'm going to take the train to Budapest. Maybe the Red Cross will take me." I knew he and Mother were friends with Alice Mercer, the director.

Apu was whistling when he entered the house a few days later, home from the capital. Within a few weeks, the Red Cross assigned him to the western front. Uneasy at leaving Mother and me on our own in Szekszárd, he arranged for us to live at the Gellért Hotel in Budapest for the duration of his absence.

Mother supervised the packing by the servants. Her makeup and jewelry went into special cases lined with rose-colored velvet. I carried my black teddy bear onto the train with me. Uncle Oli, my mother's brother, had brought it to me from Germany. I wanted to make certain the bear wouldn't be lost. Before reporting for duty, Apu traveled with us to ensure our comfort.

It was dusk when the train pulled into Budapest. The city appeared mysterious in the lengthening shadows. From the window of our horse-drawn coach which carried us to the hotel, we could see Várhegy (Castle Hill) rising in the center of town, At the top, as though crowning it, stood the neo-Baroque royal palace.

"The curving Danube flows between the two sides of the city,

Buda and Pest," Apu explained as the coach rounded a corner and the river appeared. We could see the lights on three bridges shimmering in the twilight.

"We will cross over the Lánc Hid [Chain Bridge]," Mother said, "the most beautiful of them all. I always think of it as a diamond necklace. Look, Éva! There it is."

Ahead of us was a suspension bridge lit by ornate Dickensian lamps and guarded at both ends by carved stone lions.

"It's the loveliest thing I've ever seen," I exclaimed.

"There is an old saying," Apu told us, as we rode over the bridge to the Buda side, "that the population of Budapest is divided in two, half the people live in Buda, and the other half wish they did."

The following morning, on our way to the train station to see Apu off, we heard thunder in the distance. I imagined those were guns at the front, and my heart sank. Apu's eyes glistened with tears as he hugged us good-bye and climbed onto the train. He waved to us, then faded from sight as the steam from the locomotive enveloped him. The tracks curved, the train disappeared and he was gone. Mother held tight to my hand as we left the station.

"Everyone who is able should do that, whether Christian or Jew," Mother replied, fired up with patriotism.

Although we had just left Szekszárd the day before, our town and its people seemed very far away.

The Gellért Hotel, our home for the foreseeable future, featured a cavernous lobby with high ceilings. I especially enjoyed the swimming pool with its artificial waves simulating the ocean. While in the pool for the first time, I tried to keep my balance as the swells pushed at my legs. I bumped into a girl about my age.

"Sorry," I giggled.

"It's alright," she replied, nudging me. As I landed on my fanny in the shallow water, I splashed water in the girl's face. We both laughed.

"I'm Bebe Bartók," my newfound friend informed me.

"I'm Éva Leopold."

Bebe, a bit taller than I, had a round face covered with freckles and an easygoing charm. We agreed to meet later to explore the hotel.

We quickly learned our way around the service corridors, making friends with the staff and other children who were staying at the hotel. Bebe and I spent hours peering at grown-up parties from little balconies overlooking the ballroom, and dreamed of dancing there one day. I loved riding the elevator to the dining room, so we did that over and over.

Uncle Vicci, my mother's youngest brother, had brought me a paint set from London when I was four. I delighted in splashing vibrant colors onto huge sheets of butcher paper. Now I wanted to learn to paint properly.

Mother, while sunbathing at the Gellért, fell into conversation with a French lady who offered to teach me, while also introducing me to the French language.

"Could Bebe come too?" I begged Mother when she told me about the lessons.

"I'll check with her mother," she replied.

Thus, the following Tuesday, Bebe and I, along with a cute young boy named Palcsi, went to Madame Dupont's suite for our first lesson. Madame opened a sketchbook and showed us numerous drawings, pointing out details of the human body, both in motion and in repose. Bebe and Palcsi saw right away what Madame was trying to illustrate, whereas I squinted with great determination but could not identify what she was trying to show me.

"Why don't you ask your mother for some glasses?" Bebe suggested.

"Do you think she'd let me?"

"Try this," Madame interrupted, handing me a magnifying glass. Immediately, the forms and shapes came into focus.

After class, following Bebe's suggestion, I told Mother I thought I needed glasses.

"Don't be silly," she responded. "Pretty girls don't wear glasses."

When I related Mother's reaction to Bebe, she rolled her eyes toward heaven. I shrugged my shoulders, and Bebe seemed to understand the futility of arguing with one's mother. She and I became fast friends from that moment on.

I had no trouble learning French but struggled during my art lessons, holding Madame Dupont's magnifying glass in one hand and the paintbrush in the other.

During the autumn, the hotel offered group tennis lessons after school, and Mother sent Mary to enroll me. Bebe signed up for the same class. We adored running and stretching to the limit, reaching for the ball. I even liked the sound the ball made as it vibrated my racket and the thump it made when bouncing on the asphalt.

The young instructor had us take turns standing near the lines and calling the shots. It embarrassed me in front of Bebe that I had to pretend I knew where the ball had landed though I was never quite sure. Right or wrong, Bebe seconded my decisions.

"Friends stick together," she told me after one of our lessons, and she hugged me.

As the autumn months yielded to winter, we watched the ice floes float down the Danube at sunset. They reminded me of crystal chandeliers.

Mary, frightened by the war, went back to England.

Mother hired a German woman, who insisted on being called Gretl. I hated her because she lied and blamed me for things I didn't do. Her arrival also forced me to learn German. I did learn enough to understand when she talked about Mother and me to the other governesses staying at the hotel. She said she thought Mother was jealous of my beauty. I studied my face in the mirror, but decided

Gretl was wrong. Though my face was pleasant enough and I had good skin, some freckles marched over the bridge of my nose and my hair tended to be unruly, slipping out of my braids. Mother, on the other hand, struck me as very beautiful indeed, with not a blemish in sight, nor a hair out of place.

In midwinter, my father came home from the front with typhoid fever. Children weren't allowed to visit at the hospital, so I gave Mother some pictures I had drawn and some petit fours the busboys had given me to take to Apu. I found the pictures and the sweets discarded on a room service tray near the elevator. I was devastated.

Despite my terror that Apu might be dying, he began to recover after several weeks. The doctors said he could not return to the front. Good news!

Apu wanted to stay in Budapest, so that he would have better access to war news for his newspaper columns. We moved out of the hotel into an apartment. Bebe and I vowed eternal friendship as we said good-bye. Both of us were only children, and we had become like sisters.

I remember retrieving my old box of paints—which Mother had thrown away—and clutching them, along with my teddy bear, on the way to our new apartment. Although I had turned thirteen in October, I still wanted them.

We passed through a wrought-iron gate, then walked under skeletal elm trees and along a path flanked by naked bushes. A paved walkway led us to the front door of the apartment house where we were to live.

"Look, Apu," I called to my father who was walking ahead of me, "a secret garden."

"When spring comes," he said, winking at me, "we'll have someplace to hide when we don't want our supper." He at least doesn't think me too old for childish things, I smiled to myself.

Mother sent for the servants to come up from Szekszárd, and we settled into our new home.

On November 11, 1918, Apu devoted his column to the signing of an armistice. Hungary lost nearly three-quarters of its total landmass in the peace treaty. Apu's writings in the paper described trainloads of soldiers coming home from the front. In many places, people barricaded themselves in their homes, because angry soldiers roamed the countryside, demanding food and lodging. Apu urged people to show compassion during those trying times.

In spite of my mother's disapproval, he ordered Borcsa *néni* to feed anyone who came by asking for food. If I happened to be in the kitchen at such a time, Borcsa *néni*, with a conspiratorial smile, would let me include a piece of cake or some cookies with the meal she prepared for the veterans.

One day Karcsi, our coachman, brought us a whole ham from Szekszárd. He had lost a leg in the war and was hobbling on crutches. My eyesight was so poor that I had to squint to see his face. I jumped up and hugged him, in spite of Mother's strict rules against fraternizing with servants.

When Borcsa *néni* baked the ham, the smoky flavor permeated the house. When she carved it, we were brokenhearted to discover that maggots had completely infested it.

After some months, a semblance of normalcy returned to our lives in Budapest. My parents decided it was time for me to spend a semester at a finishing school in Dresden, Germany. I wanted Mother to ask Mrs. Bartók whether Bebe could come with me, but Mother felt I should go alone, so I wouldn't have anyone with whom to speak Hungarian and would be forced to learn German.

Snow crunched under our feet as Apu and I made our way through the garden to the front gate. Apu used the excuse that he wanted to check conditions in Germany for a story he planned to write. I think he just wanted to be with me a bit longer and see my school. When we reached the street, I glanced back at our apartment, looking for a glimpse of my mother, but only Borcsa *néni* stood by the kitchen window waving. I mouthed good-bye and smiled at her, hiding my disappointment.

Having lost my way to the bathroom, Fräulein Schmidt, headmistress at the Dresden Academy for Young Ladies, berated me the very first night for being late for bed. I had taken a wrong turn along the labyrinthian gray corridors that snaked their way through the cheerless building. Fräulein Schmidt's mouth seemed permanently puckered as though she had bitten into a lemon, and I had trouble keeping a straight face while she scolded me.

My fellow students, mostly native Germans, seemed as dour as the headmistress and teased me for being an *auslander* (foreigner) when they learned I was Hungarian.

I spent two nights at the school before convincing Apu that I didn't like it and wanted to return home. On the way back, we stopped off in Munich to see a private art collection. Degas's *The Dancing Class* enchanted me, and I dreamed of painting like that someday. I was disappointed that so much of the exhibition appeared blurred to me.

I complained to Apu that I couldn't see the details, and he promptly took me to an eye specialist. At long last, I possessed my first pair of glasses.

Our next stop was in Vienna to attend the Nutcracker Ballet. "Look, Apu, snowflakes!" I exclaimed out loud. A lady sitting behind us shushed me, and I clamped my hand over my mouth. However, since I had never before seen such detail in any performance, I was thrilled.

All the way from Vienna to Budapest during our train ride, Apu kept laughing, delighted at my exclamations about things I saw for the first time.

"I've been living with a little blind mouse," my father chuckled as I read aloud the headlines on the newspapers displayed at one of the stations. "I had no idea your eyesight was so poor."

I delighted in the finely carved cherubs on our apartment house door. Mother came to meet us in the foyer.

"Where did you get those dreadful glasses?" Mother demanded.

"You know she's needed them for a long time," Apu retorted.

"They are not dreadful at all," I protested. "I can see now!"

"No more painting lessons," Mother announced, "They are ruining your eyesight."

"But I love to paint," I pleaded, addressing my remarks to my father.

"Your sight will deteriorate staring at canvases so much," Mother's remark ended the discussion.

"It's not fair," I complained.

"Sometimes life is unfair, darling," Apu cut me short. "You will still have your piano."

I knew I was defeated when Apu joined in Mother's decision. Besides, I loved my piano, so I had no choice but to settle for that.

Sixteen

In October 1921, we went to Szekszárd to celebrate my sixteenth birthday. Mother and I made elaborate plans for what was to be my first dance party.

The smell of apple strudel baking drew me to the kitchen on the afternoon of the party. When I opened the door, there was Borcsa *néni*, big white apron tied over her paisley print dress, churning the ice cream. Her sleeves were rolled up; her muscular arms glistened with perspiration. I spotted a chocolate roulade topped off with Borcsa *néni*'s famed *nagymamahaj* (granny's hair). The snow-white spun sugar glistened on top of the cake. My mother's finest china lined the counter, heaped with Viennese squares and elegant cookies, among them my favorites, dimpled with jam centers and sprinkled with powdered sugar.

"Come lick," Borcsa *néni* invited. "You may be sixteen," she chortled, "but you're not too old for ice cream." She handed me the blades of the ice cream maker, dripping with chunks of mashed peaches. I gave her a big hug and licked the blades clean.

Time seemed to stand still that day while I waited for the appointed hour for my guests to arrive. Around seven o'clock, Mary helped me slip into my rose-petal-pink flapper dress. The temperature hovered at an unseasonably warm seventy-five degrees. I worried that I would ruin the dress by perspiring.

Apu knocked on my bedroom door, hesitating before he entered. I could see him frowning.

"What's the matter? Don't you like my dress?" I asked.

"The dress is lovely," he said. "That's not the problem. Gilbert, the piano player, must have missed the train from Budapest. Karcsi came back from the train station without him," he answered.

The bad news devastated me. "Oh, darn," I exclaimed in

frustration. "I guess I'm stuck with the piano playing."

"Sorry, darling," Apu said and closed the door.

The whole party had depended on Gilbert. As the sun set, I sat down at the grand piano and began to play. My guests paired off and danced on the veranda. I had wanted so much for everything to be perfect for this party. Sixteen of my best friends were invited, some bringing dates for the first time. *Why hadn't I been allowed to continue painting? Then I would never have learned to play the piano.* The flowers in my hair wilted, along with my spirits.

As I played, couples whirled past the archway on the veranda.

I glanced up and saw my reflection in the mirror. The candles, which my mother had placed on the piano, outlined my face, and light from the flames reflected in my eyes and hair. Mother had lent me a long strand of pearls that I had knotted on my chest to accentuate my breasts. *Am I truly beautiful?* I wondered. Apu had said so. Mother, on the other hand, had glanced at me wearing her pearls and nodded.

"It will do," she had said. I felt she didn't like it when Apu complimented my appearance.

"Palcsi has become a handsome young man," Mother commented, appearing at my elbow by the piano, just as Palcsi led Bebe out onto the veranda.

"He's all right," I replied, not wanting to encourage Mother's matchmaking.

Bebe, Palcsi, and I had remained friends ever since the painting lessons at the Gellért Hotel. Palcsi was the only one of us still studying art.

Bebe looked very grown up, in a red flapper dress, with her jet-black hair drawn up in curls on top of her head.

Though I enjoyed being around boys, I had no special interest in any particular one.

Bebe came to stand by the piano a little later, between dances.

"I've met a boy in Budapest..."

Suddenly, we were interrupted by the sound of violins—gypsy music—coming from the dark garden below. We hurried out to the veranda and looked over the stone wall. My father had hired a gypsy band! I ran to slam the piano shut. For the rest of the evening, I took turns dancing with all the boys.

Surrounded by good friends, enveloped by the soulful music and breathing the fragrance of late-blooming roses from the garden, I was delighted. Bebe whispered to me that she was in love.

"What is his name?" I managed to ask her before my partner spun me away from Bebe.

"Laci Jakus," she purred.

Stars twinkled overhead. My guests and I ate peach ice cream and drank champagne. It was a night from a storybook. Even now, more than sixty years later, I can close my eyes and hear the haunting gypsy melodies of that long-ago, blissful night.

Mother, like many Hungarians, admired the British for their impeccable manners and sophistication. My parents gave me a birthday gift of a six-week trip to England, hoping that some of the British gentility would rub off on me. The following summer, I stayed as a paying guest in the home of a vicar and his wife in Cornwall.

Every morning, the vicar appeared for breakfast, and, still standing, before saying grace, would turn to his wife.

"How is His Majesty this morning?" he'd inquire, referring to the ailing King George.

His wife then gave him the latest medical bulletin from the wireless. Only then could we all sit down and have our meal. The British people seemed to regard their royal family as part of their own. I made a mental note to relate all this to Mother when I returned home, to add to her collection of trivia about England.

Gwen, a young governess hired by the vicar, accompanied me

everywhere. I perfected my English while she and I took many day trips to explore Cornwall and walked for hours in the countryside, followed by tea in little country inns.

When I turned seventeen, my parents and I traveled from Budapest to a lakeside Swiss resort frequented by British tourists in the Bergen Valley. Mother delighted in being surrounded by English speakers.

"Let's sign up for the tennis tournament, Éva," Mother enthused on our first morning at the hotel. I hadn't played in several months, so I was a bit reluctant, but I agreed, just to please her. I double-faulted right away in my first match.

"Look out, Éva!" Apu yelled from the stands during my opponent's initial serve. The ball grazed my left elbow. I hadn't seen it coming. Mother had told me not to wear my glasses in public, so I was trying to play without them.

At forty-two, Mother outshone all the younger players. In her deciding match and final play, she made the most of her chance with a sliced overhead that landed on the line and put the finishing touch on her flawless game. She had easily won the tournament.

That evening, participants were crowded into the dining room as we entered. Lighted candles reflected in the mirrors lining the walls. Mother, looking radiant in a pale pink full-length gown, made me feel underdressed in the flapper dress I had worn for my sixteenth birthday. Everyone stood and toasted her. The orchestra played "Tales from the Vienna Woods," her favorite waltz. Apu, looking splendid in his tuxedo, escorted Mother onto the dance floor as the onlookers clapped. She loved every minute of it. I had lost in the first round of the tournament, and I suspect my mother relished that too! For once it was perfectly clear which of us was number one.

The following week, the Lener Quartet, a very famous musical ensemble founded in Budapest in 1918, played at our hotel. I sat for hours every evening listening to the classical music.

"Playing an instrument is not an intellectual exercise, Éva," my piano teacher, Nagy *néni,* had told me. When I listened to Hedric, the violinist in the quartet, I realized for the first time what she meant when she had added, "You have to feel the music in your nerve endings and in your gut."

The musicians had a well-deserved reputation for excellence, and were also known for being the ugliest men anyone had ever seen. However, Hedric, who happened to be Hungarian, had soulful brown eyes and wavy chestnut hair that brushed his shirt collar and made me want to run my fingers through it.

The night of their last performance at the hotel, I waited until the musicians packed up their instruments, walked off the stage, and headed for the exit. For the first time, I realized that Hedric was shorter than I, and as he came close to where I was sitting, I noticed that he had a bulbous nose.

"Excuse me." I gathered up the courage to speak to him. "The Dvořák Piano Quartet sounded superb," I said, attempting sophisticated small talk.

Clearly he considered me too young to bother with; he just gave me an absent-minded smile. "Thank you, miss," he replied, brushing past me as he left the room. His cologne lingered and I sighed.

Early in September every year, the mists came up the Bergen Valley and people started to leave. We packed for home.

Hedric will come to perform in Budapest in the autumn, I thought, but I never saw him again.

Jóska

In October 1922, my cousin Ágota (Agatha) gave a dance party.
Though I had turned seventeen and had been invited, my mother
was reluctant to let me go. Up until that time, I had never been to
a party where my mother had not controlled the guest list. After an
uphill battle, she relented.

Mother wouldn't let me pin up my hair, so I just wore a
brown velvet ribbon in it and put on a new, pale-pink silken dress.
I had wanted it to be grass green, but Mother insisted on pink, her
favorite color.

When we arrived at the party, people were already dancing.
I noticed a young man, sitting in the largest armchair, with girls
perched on each arm. Two others stood behind, bending over him,
and two sat at his feet. He had combed his chestnut-brown hair
straight back, parted on the side. I judged him to be in his mid-
twenties and quite sophisticated. He appeared well aware of his good
looks. The girls laughed at whatever he said. He sat tall and straight
in the armchair, thoroughly at ease, and for just an instant his bright
blue eyes held my gaze.

I moved into the shadows, curious, wanting to hear what made the girls laugh. I knew I was just as beautiful as any of them, but I didn't want to be an armchair ornament.

The girls surrounding the man all talked at once, and he was grinning. I caught half a sentence of his, directed at the entire group, saying something like "One at a time." Then, turning his attention to the prettiest girl sitting on an arm of the chair, he said, "It's hot in here. You can start fanning me now."

Most girls carried fans in colors that matched their chartreuse, buttercup, and lilac-shaded dresses. *How impertinent*, I thought. *I can't stand these handsome guys. They are all the same. They think they are God's gift to all creation.* My mother, who hoped to marry me off at an early age, would, I am sure, have liked it if I had demurely joined the group at this man's feet. I caught her glancing toward me from across the room, ignored her, and headed for the buffet.

Later, while I danced with my artist friend, Palcsi, the man who had been surrounded by all those girls, cut in. Palcsi and I had been discussing the current exhibit at the National Museum. While I was by no means an intellectual, since that was regarded as deadly to one's marriage prospects, I did love art and music.

"I'm Jóska Badics," he said, dipping me in an exaggerated dance step. I started to introduce myself, but he said, "Éva, it's my business to know such beauty."

Much to my embarrassment, I felt myself blushing. He danced well but made silly small talk that was not nearly as interesting as my discussion with Palcsi had been. Jóska spoke of fox hunting, the weather, and his brothers' exploits with women. I had a hunch they were Jóska's exploits.

My dance card had been filled at the start of the evening, before I met Jóska, so he kept cutting in. Whenever I danced with someone else, he stared at me from the other side of the room. I was flattered by all the attention but uncomfortable at the same time.

During the ride home in a taxi, my mother said she hadn't caught his name. I told her Jóska Bakics or something like that. "He is so handsome," Mother said, "and has such wonderful manners." I made a mental note that he must have spent some time buttering up my mother.

"I guess so," I said. "It's a pity he is so dumb."

"He's from an aristocratic family, studying for his doctorate in agriculture, you know," Mother continued, giving me information she had gleaned at the party. Not wanting to bolster her fantasies, I didn't respond.

From then on, it was phone call after phone call. Jóska even arranged dancing lessons at a studio for us. On Sunday afternoons, we went as part of a group of young friends, but I didn't pay much attention to him, not wanting to encourage him. Then he started lending me books on history that he had particularly enjoyed, and I began to realize he had a more serious side. He tended to be late for various events and sometimes, when he promised to be there, didn't show up at all. He seemed to have good and bad sides to his personality.

One day Jóska came to our house and left some photos for me. I was having a piano lesson and didn't see him. He called that evening, and when I picked up the phone, he sounded very serious.

"You know, Éva, you saved my life today." I could tell by his voice that for once he wasn't joking.

"Why, what happened?" I asked.

"I was supposed to go with my brother Aurél in a plane, on a flight around Budapest. Aurél had told me it would be one of the very first such flights. I arrived too late for the takeoff because I had dropped off those pictures to you. Aurél missed it too, waiting for me at the airfield. When I got there, the plane had just taken off. Something went wrong. It just wasn't gaining enough altitude. I watched as it headed right for the trees at the end of the runway.

Then it exploded. Aurél and I tried to get near it, but the whole thing was engulfed in flames. Everyone on board died."

"Oh, Jóska, how dreadful." I realized I felt very glad he wasn't one of them.

Although my family lived in Szekszárd during most of 1923, we spent the winter in Budapest. I worked hard at my piano, preparing for my first examination at the Academy of Music. Rachmaninoff, Mozart, and Chopin held great attraction for me. Jóska flattered me by telling me how well I played and would stand outside in the street to listen when I practiced. As so often happened, however, when I was enthused about something, Mother tried to pour cold water on it all.

"Don't listen to Jóska. Your hands aren't strong enough," she told me one day while I struggled with a particularly difficult piece.

"It's got nothing to do with strength. I'm just having trouble with the tempo," I told her.

"If you had the talent, you'd have it right by now," she concluded, leaving me furious.

Whether I had enough talent to be great remained to be seen. My teachers at the academy thought I should train as a concert pianist. I figured that my mother said nasty things about my abilities because she couldn't play at all.

If Mother, a very strong, highly intelligent person, had been born in a later time, she could have been an executive, a writer, or anything she might have wanted to be. As it was, she was relegated to playing endless rounds of bridge or tennis and fussing with the house at Szekszárd. She kept our home in perfect condition and frequently remodeled it. Frustrated by the lack of a more meaningful outlet for her talents, much of her boundless energy was channeled toward me. Though she almost always won the bridge games and the tennis matches, and the house gleamed, she was not quite so successful in bending me to her will.

In 1924, my parents bought a big house in Budapest and decided to keep the one in Szekszárd for holidays. Our new home, a spacious, airy beauty, had big picture windows to let in lots of light. It even had a salon, expensively furnished to accommodate Mother's bridge club. Next to the salon was Apu's study, with floor-to-ceiling mahogany bookcases all around, which provided him with quiet solitude for his writing.

I had the only room on the third floor, where I could be alone, and even paint sometimes, though I wasn't supposed to because of my poor vision. The piano—which was in the living room—kept me under my mother's watchful eye most of the time.

I went to many dances and to various country houses for hunting parties, occasions generally engineered by Jóska. Though I didn't care much for the dances, they provided us the opportunity to be together. We often examined the book collections in our hosts' libraries. We loved to eat in restaurants and go to concerts, the opera, and the theater. My mother often watched me dress before these outings and commented that I was underweight. Since I could swim, ski, and play tennis for hours, I decided that I was healthy and it didn't matter that I was thin. My mother, by then in her forties, was a bit plump, and it occurred to me that perhaps she was a little jealous.

Jobs were scarce, but Jóska had managed to find part-time work as an assistant to the curator at the Agricultural Museum while continuing to study for his doctorate.

One night, as Jóska and I were walking toward the opera house, a beggar approached us.

"How is the world treating you?" Jóska asked him before the man had a chance to ask for money.

"My gout is acting up, my wife died, and I've been thrown out of my apartment, sir," he replied, delighted that someone was taking an interest in him.

"Go to Mr. Király, at the gatekeeper's cottage at the

Agricultural Museum, and tell him Mr. Badics sent you. Tell him I said to give you a place to sleep tonight. I'll see you in the morning," Jóska said, handing the beggar a five-forint note.

"God bless you, sir," the man stammered, delighted with his good fortune. Jóska bade him good night, and we entered the opera house. It was typical of him to address the beggar directly and not just give him a handout.

It made me proud of Jóska that he could never pass up anyone in need. He would often bring home various unsavory characters who were down on their luck and insist that they be fed or housed or both. I, in turn, learned from him to respect even the least fortunate.

Jóska always made it a point to be solicitous toward my mother. He asked about her health and activities whenever he saw her.

Mother, in turn, grew very fond of Jóska. She decided to give a party for his twenty-fourth birthday. The guest list grew to a hundred people. "I didn't know you were a hundred," I teased him, referring to a custom of matching the number of guests with the age of the celebrant at family parties.

Jóska had conned Borcsa *néni* into baking him a *Dobos Torte*. This cake, made up of no fewer than twenty-four layers with a chocolate cream filling, was capped with a burnt sugar topping and twenty-four candles. I sat next to Jóska at dinner and, over the glow of those twenty-four candles, he whispered to me that he loved me. Somewhat taken aback, as I was only eighteen and not in love with him, I made light of his remarks.

"I'm much too young to be serious about anyone."

"There is no hurry, but I know you will be my wife. I knew it from the first moment I set eyes on you," Jóska told me later that evening, while dancing with me.

His blue eyes shone as he looked at me. He twirled me into the small entryway off the living room as the music stopped. While keeping one arm around me, with a fluid movement he put his middle and index fingers under my chin, and gently lifted my face to his and kissed me. His lips aroused feelings in me that I had not experienced before.

"I am going skating with George in the morning. He is tall, dark and handsome—my type of man," I stammered.

Jóska just laughed.

Whenever we met he gazed at me. Not unlike other young men, he would sneak the occasional kiss, which always left me a bit more unsettled than when anyone else kissed me.

I met several of Jóska's five brothers. They turned up everywhere I went and appeared to be following me around. The family's intelligence network was superb. Jóska knew my every move. I sneaked onto the streetcar one day without paying the fare. That very same day, this information was relayed by Jóska's only sister Juci to Jóska's mother, who had never even met me. Juci had recognized me from a picture Jóska had shown her and had followed me onto the streetcar. Another one of the brothers told his parents that although I looked lovely, I also appeared to be sickly thin.

Jóska's unceasing attentions paid off. Slowly, imperceptibly, he became part of my consciousness. I caught myself looking for him in crowds. One night, I dreamed of us dancing: I was wearing an Alice-blue gown. He twirled me round and round, out onto the veranda and under shooting stars he told me that he loved me. When I awoke I realized that I loved him, too.

According to custom, Jóska and I went everywhere with a group and had little time to ourselves. One afternoon, some friends joined us to go ice-skating at an amusement park on the *Margit Sziget*, an island in the middle of the Danube. It was late afternoon on a brisk winter day.

"Let's go ride the Ferris wheel!" Jóska said as soon as we arrived at the park. His glance warmed me in spite of the cold winter breeze.

He reached over and gently wrapped my red wool scarf across my throat and over my right shoulder.

I looked around to include some of our friends, but Jóska grabbed my hand and said, "Just us," as he pulled me away from the rink.

I ran with him, and we boarded the ride just before the wheel began turning. When we reached the highest point, the Ferris wheel stopped. We were suspended way up high, overlooking Budapest. The lights from the bridges on the Danube sparkled beneath us, and sounds of gypsy music drifted up from the skating rink. I looked at Jóska and found him smiling at me.

"Got you alone at last," he said as he reached for my hand.

I looked down to see why the Ferris wheel had stopped, and could see the little man who operated it grinning up at us. I realized Jóska must have arranged for him to stop the wheel when our seat reached the crest of the ride.

"Marry me?" Jóska asked and started digging in his pockets. "I know it's here somewhere," he said. He produced a little green velvet-covered box from his shirt pocket and handed it to me. I popped it open. The colored lights hanging above us on the Ferris wheel glimmered back at me from a diamond, set in a white gold band. I wanted this moment to last forever. Jóska lifted the ring from its box and, though I had not answered his initial question (he seemed to require no answer), I slipped the ring on my finger.

I thought the earth was moving as Jóska's arms closed around me and he kissed me. I opened my eyes and realized it was not the earth, but only the Ferris wheel. I reluctantly slipped the ring off and put it back in the box.

"Let's keep our engagement a secret for now, Jóska," I said. "It will be a while before we can marry. Secrecy will save us from having to answer prying questions from well-meaning friends."

"I wish I could marry you tomorrow," he replied.

Jóska's wages at the time barely met his own expenses. We knew we had to wait another four years for him to finish his doctoral studies before we could be married.

From that day on, we were together whenever possible. Jóska often met me after my piano lesson, and we would walk around for a while, going home slowly and circuitously. There were endless group outings, walks in the hills, more dancing lessons; we invented all manner of excuses to be together.

Because we couldn't go anywhere unchaperoned, in December 1925 Jóska invited my parents to accompany us to a Viennese ball being held at the Technical University where he studied.

I wore a Grecian style, deep-rose taffeta gown, with a half-inch gold trim outlining the top, cut to reveal one shoulder. Apu played the "Blue Danube Waltz" on the record player when Jóska, who looked dashing in a tuxedo, came to pick us up. As soon as he saw me, he held out his hands, took me in his arms, and danced me around our foyer. He kept whispering, "Beautiful, beautiful Éva," in my ear, in between making conversation with my parents over my shoulder. He told Mother she looked stunning.

At the ball, he flirted with the women and bantered with the men, showing interest in everyone.

In the course of the four years of our engagement, Jóska and I learned to know each other very well. He was that fascinating combination: extremely popular and fond of social activities of all kinds, and yet deep down, a very private person, independent of anyone, an individualist and, in a way, even a loner. He reminded me of the Kipling lines, "I am the cat that walks by himself, and all places are alike to me." I learned that he resented what he regarded as prying questions, any sign of what he deemed to be interference in his life.

The years of schooling passed, and Jóska received his doctorate. He graduated summa cum laude and was given a fellowship to teach for a year in Switzerland. We needed my parents' consent for me to marry at twenty-two, since in Hungary twenty-four was the age of majority. Luckily, Mother saw no point in prolonging our secret engagement. My parents decided to give us a monthly allowance, so that along with Jóska's stipend, we would have enough on which to live.

According to custom, Jóska and I announced our engagement at a party attended by all my girlfriends, and I started wearing my beautiful ring. Borcsa *néni* baked a ring into a cake: the girl who found it in the slice she was served would be the next bride. Bebe let out a whoop when she bit into her piece. She and her Laci would follow us down the aisle four months later.

My father wrote a beautiful poem for me in honor of our special day, ending with the words, "*Csak egy kislány van a világon*" (There is only one little girl in the world).

Although both my parents were fond of Jóska, especially my mother, Apu hated the thought of my leaving home. My mother, on the other hand, resented, at least a little, all the attention my father heaped upon me, and had a soft spot in her heart for the man who would be taking her daughter off her hands.

I had wanted a forest-green evening gown for a very long time, but my dresses had to be pink, pink, pink throughout the years because that was Mother's favorite color. At last, for my engagement party, I had my way.

"Why don't you let the young lady tell us what she would like?" the *couturière* asked Mother. I don't think that thought had occurred to Mother, but she agreed.

Perhaps Gretl, the German governess, had been right after all—about my being more beautiful than my mother.

The Wedding

Vestiges of summer drifted through my open bedroom window the night before our wedding in September 1926. Fragrant roses still bloomed under my window, the white blossoms illuminated by the full moon. After our years of engagement, I felt I was going home. Home to me ever after would be with Jóska. To this day, some sixty years later, so it has proved to be.

"This marriage will depend on you," Mother greeted me at breakfast on my wedding day. Meaning, I suppose, that I'd better mend my ways. I had been, all things said and done, a somewhat spoiled only child, but did she need to remind me of that just then?

Some roadwork delayed us as my father and I were being driven to the church.

Mother, riding in a separate car with some of the bridesmaids, arrived ahead of us. Believing that Apu and I were right behind her, she told the bridesmaids to start their procession down the aisle. They did as she directed, reached the altar, and took their places to the side of the priest.

Expecting my entrance, the organist restarted the wedding march. Everybody waited in vain for the bride. Jóska later told me that those few minutes had seemed like an eternity as he stood by the front pew with all eyes on him.

When Apu and I arrived at the church, I felt calm and happy. I noticed right away, however, that—contrary to our arrangements—the organist was playing Mendelssohn's wedding march instead of Lohengrin's. When my father and I began our slow walk up the aisle, I looked toward the front of the church. There stood Jóska. His expression told me that he was unaware of the change in music.

He appeared completely self-possessed; he, too, was coming home. As required by law, we had already been married at the registrar's office the day before in a civil ceremony.

"You know I'll be happy to divorce you anytime. This is not bondage," Jóska had declared afterward, half-jokingly. I had been a bit taken aback, to say the least.

"So would I," said I, not to be outdone, though shocked at the very thought of what he had said. So, what was there to be nervous about? I could always go back to being single.

As I walked down the aisle, Jóska regarded me with a yearning glance that delighted me. I hoped no one else noticed.

I wore an ivory-shaded taffeta gown with a scalloped neckline. A beaded headband secured my Spanish lace veil with an eight-foot train, carried by Jóska's young niece and nephew. A simple strand of pearls encircled my throat. I held a bouquet of cascading white orchids.

The six bridesmaids wore cornflower-blue taffeta gowns, with form-fitting tops and bell-shaped skirts. They carried bouquets of cornflowers and forget-me-nots. Jóska and the ushers were in traditional black.

I remember only a few of the priest's words from the ceremony. He told us to tread the paths of life and lapsed into his ancestral German, *"Mitt einander, nicht neben einander"* (Together, not just side by side).

The organ nearly inaudible; the scent of jasmine, lilac, and incense; the light through the beautiful stained glass windows; and "'til death do us part"—I remember only this.

On our way out, Évi, Jóska's three-year-old niece, dropped my train and ran to her mother, leaving her brother Bélus, aged five, to carry it by himself.

When we returned to my parents' home for the reception, Borcsa *néni*, who by then had been with our family for more than half a century, was standing in the sunlit garden. She wanted to catch a glimpse of us before she had to serve the buffet. She couldn't speak, she was so moved. With tears in her eyes, she stroked the sleeve of my taffeta gown.

"Borcsa *néni*, I think we'd better go in now. The rest of them will be here any minute," I chided.

Jóska stopped me—laying a hand on my arm.

"There's no hurry, Borcsa *néni*," he said to her. "You look at her as long as you want."

His lightning grasp of the way the other person felt and kind responses were characteristics I had not fully understood until we were actually together all the time. I learned to love Jóska all the more for it.

In those days of virginal brides, most were too nervous to eat at their own reception. I felt completely at ease with Jóska and anticipated our wedding night with joy.

The buffet was marvelous, and several elderly aunts looked scandalized when they saw me eating. Then I went up to my room to change.

When I reappeared wearing a Chantilly silk dress, a gasp could be heard from those assembled.

At an unguarded moment, I caught a look of unbridled passion in Jóska's eyes. I quickened my pace, tossing my bouquet over the banister as I flew down the last few steps. Jóska grabbed my hand and whispered, "I love you! Let's get out of here."

We ran out the door, through the garden and into our waiting car. Jóska drove with one hand on the wheel and one ever so slightly touching my thigh. I could not trust my voice to speak, so sat perfectly still as we wound our way off the Gellért hill, away from my childhood. We were to spend our wedding night at the Gellért Hotel.

Twilight was descending on Budapest by the time we checked in, and Jóska led me through our room onto the balcony. The lights of the parliament building across the Danube reflected in the river, and the Chain Bridge glittered below us. Jóska lifted my face to his with two fingers of his right hand and kissed me with such gentleness that I began to tingle. His other arm enveloped me and drew me to him.

Hours later, the sound of violins drifted up from one of the ballrooms and invaded our consciousness. Jóska whispered, "Would my wife care to go downstairs and dance with me?"

"Only if you promise to kiss me after every dance," I answered. He reached for my chin with those two magic fingers once again.

We kissed and dressed and kissed some more. I put on a sea green voile gown, which unbeknown to Mother, Apu had bought for me on our last trip to Vienna. Jóska stood behind me, gazing at me in the mirror as I fixed my hair. "Let this never end," he said quietly, as though speaking to himself.

He led me into the ballroom. A remarkable stillness descended on the crowd, and all eyes turned in our direction. The band struck up a Viennese waltz as Jóska took me in his arms and whirled me around the dance floor. I caught a quick glimpse of two little girls peeking over a small balcony, but the next time I looked they were gone. I remembered those innocent childhood days during the Great War when I had spent hours on that very balcony observing the parties below. A glance at Jóska brought me back to the present, and I echoed his earlier words: "Let this never end."

Jóska and Éva on
Terrace at Cservölgy

And We Lived Happily Ever After

For a wedding present, my parents deeded us a two hundred
acre farm hidden in the midst of an oak forest in the rolling hill
country southwest of Budapest. Cservölgy (the Valley of the Oaks)
had been in my father's family for generations. A mansion built of
native stone stood on one of the hills overlooking the property. A
large veranda dominated the facade of the house from which Lake
Balaton, the biggest lake in Hungary, could be seen in the distance.
The interior of the house was reminiscent of my parents' home in
Szekszárd—airy, light, and comfortable.

Jóska replaced the crops on the farm with an experimental
fruit orchard, and we spent many hours riding horses to oversee the
work in progress. We learned to love every knoll and gully on the
property, and we talked for hours of plans for the future.

Servants, whose husbands worked in the fields, ran the
household under my direction. Often, in the evenings, we sent
them home early. Once we were alone, Jóska would light the fire in
the living room fireplace. We stretched out on the deep pile rug in

front of it and listened to romantic music on the phonograph or the radio. He frequently reached over and cupped my face in his hands, kissed me, and told me that he loved me. Our lives became more and more enmeshed over the years.

By the 1930s, Cservölgy became the center of our universe and the place we thought of as home.

Although some people in Budapest were concerned with the coming to power of Hitler in Germany, few officials or religious leaders grasped that a radical new form of evil had entered the world.

My life from early childhood had been secular, but I had absorbed the Catholic culture that had surrounded me. I felt not even a twinge of personal concern. At Cservölgy, Hitler seemed very far away.

Our house sat on a hill like a queen on a throne, above the handful of homes occupied by the peasants who worked for us.

The life cycle of the seasons determined our activities. We spent the summers at Cservölgy, always conscious of the passing clouds, since the timing of the harvest of various crops and fruits depended a great deal on the vagaries of the weather.

A deep hole in a shaded area outside the kitchen door was filled with ice by the workmen during the winter. The ice kept our food cold most of the summer. Occasional bouts of dysentery were suffered by members of the household and sometimes our guests and served to remind us of the imperfection of this system of refrigeration.

In her late sixties by this time, Borcsa *néni* whom Mother had passed on to us as a wedding present, reacted to the primitive conditions at Cservölgy by saying, "For you, my dear child, and for Dr. Jóska, I can do anything."

Much to my delight and my mother's despair, Borcsa *néni* continued to address me as her dear child until her dying day. Mother thought our relationship was much too informal for a mistress and her cook. But Borcsa *néni* took command of our kitchen and brewed numerous vats of bubbling sauces and preserved fruits and vegetables for the winter. Not even my mother dared criticize her to her face.

Streams of visitors, friends and relatives alike, came to occupy the bedrooms that lined the upstairs hallway. The household often swelled to twenty people on a weekend.

Jóska spent his days overseeing the work of the peasants, checking to see that gypsy encampments did not encroach on our property, talking to beggars passing through the countryside, and seeing to a 101 details every day.

I remember my young cousin Stephen coming often. He, a lanky redheaded youngster, ten years Jóska's junior, shared Jóska's love of the outdoors and was fascinated by his exploits. The two of them would go off for a day or two, stalking stags in the oak forest surrounding the property.

"We walked over the top of a fox's lair," Stephen related with great excitement when they returned from one of their forays. "You wouldn't believe the stench, Éva."

Another time they came home with four baby squirrels. "You can take a couple of them home," Jóska told Stephen. A few days later, Stephen reported that the two had escaped down the wall of their five-story apartment building in Budapest, one of them taking up residence in the park across the street.

"I managed to capture Cumpy—that's what I named the other one. I caught him on the balcony of the flat two floors down from us."

Another time when Stephen came to visit, he asked if he could ride one of the horses.

"You can give Négus a try," Jóska told him, not expecting Stephen to rise to the challenge. Stephen didn't realize that the Négus Jóska was talking about was a strapping young mule of two summers, standing fifteen hands high. The animal was black as his namesake, the emperor of Abyssinia, and just as wild.

"Négus dumped me unceremoniously, Éva," Stephen related. "I'll try him again tomorrow."

On that same visit, Stephen and Jóska discussed various names for our new wire-haired fox terrier puppy.

"I know the perfect name for him," Jóska exclaimed. "Kleby, since he's foxy!" He alluded to Klebelsberg, whom everyone knew as Kleby. He was the Hungarian education minister at the time, and my father-in-law's boss.

"Kleby it shall be!" I laughed in delight.

Although Jóska and I weren't rich, we belonged to the aristocracy. His family had been given a title by the king in the fourteenth century. Jóska wore a signet ring with the family crest, shaped like a shield, engraved with the tower of a castle, a dove of peace, and a crown, on the ring finger of his right hand. In spite of our status, sometimes we needed to hock the silver to tide us over until the harvest came in.

In 1934, we anticipated the birth of our first child. By tradition, in those days a great deal of emphasis was placed on the firstborn son. Jóska came from a family that bore various titles (which could only be passed on through male children) bestowed by the king of Hungary back in 1300.

We were fleetingly disappointed when the baby turned out to be a girl. With some reluctance on my part, at Jóska's urging, we named her "Livia," after my mother. Jóska proceeded to treat little Livia as though she had been a son. He threw her into the air, roughhoused with her, and brought her toy trucks.

"I'll teach you to hunt next week," he said to her when she was six months old, making me laugh. I visualized our delicate baby toting a rifle. Livia, in turn, trailed after Jóska the minute she could manage to crawl fast enough.

Shortly after Livia's birth in 1934, Hitler's power began to increase. The threat of a Nazi takeover of Germany and the eventual annexation of Hungary became a real possibility. We in Hungary nonetheless firmly believed for years that "it couldn't happen here." The news from Germany, however, was such that Jóska and I agreed that if Livia had not already been born, we would have decided not to have any children.

Because of my own longing over the years for a sibling, I long ago had decided that if I had children, I would have more than one. So regardless of the menacing political situation in Germany, I became pregnant again.

Our second child was born just before Christmas in 1936. As I came out from under the anesthetic, a nurse joyously announced that we had a baby girl. I burst into tears, feeling like a failure for once again not having provided Jóska with the longed-for son.

We named the baby after my favorite cousin, Ágota (Agatha). It was not until two days later on Christmas Eve that Ági (Aggie), as she later became known, and I became friends. I had opened the window of my hospital room to let in some fresh air and bundled up the baby against the chill. As the first church bells started to peal across the Buda hills, calling people to midnight mass, Ágota clutched my finger, opened her eyes, and smiled at me. Over the years, many wise people have tried to convince me that two-day-old infants don't smile, but I know better.

Due to our growing family, Jóska and I decided to take in paying guests at Cservölgy during the summers to help meet expenses. Some of the guests caused a good deal of trouble.

One day while I was looking after the children at the swimming pool, Kati, our maid, came running out of the house, wide-eyed and breathless.

"Madam, that lady who just arrived with her husband"—Kati paused for a moment to regain her composure—"she's turned all the pictures toward the wall. She told me she couldn't stand to look at them."

"I'll deal with it, Kati," I told her. "Take the children to their room, please."

Orchard at Cservölgy

Livia at Cservögy 1938

Ági as an Infant

When I entered the house and located the woman's husband, he informed me that his wife had just been released from a mental institution. I suggested he take her home to Budapest where she would be in familiar surroundings.

"I didn't think the pictures were that bad," Jóska laughed, when I told him what had happened. We agreed that having strangers in the house wasn't worth it, and from then on, we would only allow people referred by friends and family to stay with us.

In addition to the farm, Jóska and I kept a three-bedroom apartment in the Vár (Palace) District of Budapest. Once the harvest was in, we left Cservölgy and annually returned to the city in time for the symphony and opera season.

In the spring of 1939, an elegantly dressed, diminutive woman who identified herself as Mrs. Pici rang the doorbell of our apartment. She had clipped our ad from the previous year's newspaper and asked if we were still accepting vacationers. She felt from the description that Cservölgy was very much the type of place she and her husband were looking for, peaceful and quiet.

Margit Pici explained that her husband András had just retired from the army. I recognized the name from the caption of a memorable newspaper photo of a rugged-looking officer, resplendent in dress-white uniform, on the occasion of his promotion to four-star general.

Jóska and I talked over Mrs. Pici's request and decided we would make an exception. The Picis came, and for the next four years they stayed with us for six to eight weeks every summer.

In July 1939, when Ági was two-and-a-half years old, we decided she had acquired sufficient table manners to join the family and our guests for meals. András and Margit Pici had arrived for their stay and were fond of the children. The couple, having married late in life, had none of their own.

At dinner one evening, I asked Kati to extend the dining room table with an extra leaf and put Ági's highchair to my right. Kati set a place for General Pici on the other side of Ági. Everything went smoothly. Jóska and András, seated at the far end of the table, were deep in conversation about the latest news coming from Germany. András had his left elbow on the table as he leaned toward Jóska.

I glanced at Ági, pleased that she appeared to be observing András as though absorbed in what he was saying.

"Elbow, elbow, General," Ági suddenly declared, as she reached over to remove the offending arm from the table. Livia, sitting on my left, giggled.

"Sorry, András," I said.

"It's I who must apologize to this young lady." András winked at Ági as he said this. "I'm forgetting my manners," he went on, smiling at the children.

"You've taught your sister well," said Margit, sitting to Livia's left and leaning toward her.

Although András was lame, having taken a bullet in one leg during the Great War, he nevertheless went for long walks with Jóska. Jóska often had Ági piggybacked on his shoulders while Livia trailed along behind the two men. Jóska and András sometimes reappeared from these excursions with each carrying one of the children.

Cukor (Sugar), a beautiful old komondor—a large, powerful, shaggy-coated sheepdog—was part of the household that summer. Cukor became very sick. The horses were overworked, so Jóska hoped to cure the dog without the necessity of taking him by horse-drawn wagon to the veterinarian in the village three kilometers away.

I went downstairs late at night to check on the dog and found András sitting on the floor in front of the entrance to the cellar with the dog's head on his lap. "I'm just keeping him company," András said. "Cukor is going to pull through," he added. And he did.

Margit, a friendly person, former teacher, and a model military wife, thought highly of her husband. Both of them were very interested in politics and world affairs, as were we. Margit once told me András could do a better job running the country than anyone in government she had ever met.

Margit must have been very lovely in her younger days. Even in her fifties, she had a regal figure and dressed beautifully, often in powder blue. I remember her at our New Year's Eve party in 1939, resplendent in black, with a lovely décolleté. When midnight came, András went up to her and kissed first her hand and then her cheek.

For several years, we fell into the habit of inviting Bebe and Laci Jakus, who had married shortly after Jóska and I, to stay at Cservölgy at the same time that Margit and András vacationed there.

Laci Jakus, a clean-cut man Jóska's age with a similar air of self-assurance, shared Jóska's interests in hunting and agriculture. He, Jóska, and the Picis were all ardent bridge players, often spending the languid summer evenings locked in fierce competition on the veranda. Bebe and I, not too keen on the game, were relieved that the four of them seemed so compatible, leaving us to relax in lounge chairs and catch up on each other's lives.

On occasion, Jóska became somewhat of a Marine sergeant, directing everyone in various activities such as horseback expeditions and picnics. One day, since we had more guests than horses, he asked me to ride our mule Böske. He had named the animal after my gentle aunt, my cousin Stephen's mother. I, having dropped out of riding school somewhere between learning the trot and the gallop, hadn't the faintest idea how to control this stubborn creature. In short order, the mule threw me in the middle of a plowed field.

"Catch him and ride him home," Jóska shouted when he saw I was unhurt. He rode off with his guests. I managed to catch Böske, who had stopped to graze, and to ride him home successfully, very pleased with myself.

Jóska was very popular with just about everyone. The house was always full of company. Women paid him undue attention, fawning over him. Usually he seemed to take little notice of them. Sometimes there was a short-term "interlude." Though hurt, I didn't worry too much. I never felt I had purchased a slave. I wanted him to be completely free to do as he pleased. This, of course, was because I always knew that I was "the Woman" in his life.

We understood each other very well. Months would go by without the slightest friction. Jóska had a wonderful sense of humor and could always cheer me up if needed.

"There is peace at your house," Laci remarked one day. "You don't often find that when visiting people." I was glad.

My ancestors had tried with varying degrees of success to improve conditions for the peasants on the farm. When I was a child, Apu continued these efforts by providing outhouses. Since time immemorial, those who tilled our soil had relieved themselves in the woods. Apu ordered the structures to be built after the harvest had been gathered. He made a special trip to the farm in the middle of winter to inspect the new facilities. When he returned to Budapest, he related that there had been a snowstorm the night before he arrived at Cservölgy. As he approached the farm by horse-drawn sleigh, he could see the outhouses and footprints in the snow leading toward them. He felt a warm glow knowing what a good thing he had done for the workers. As he neared the outhouses, to his amazement, he saw that the footprints did not stop at the new facilities, but continued on up to the woods, where they had always gone. It took another generation before the peasants accepted these modern conveniences. The coming of collectivization, under the Russian occupation, later brought indoor plumbing to the workers at Cservölgy. We at the big house, on the other hand, had flush toilets as far back as I can remember.

From a very young age, I had nagging doubts about our privileged life. Among other niceties, I felt uncomfortable about the fact that someone else had to waken at four o'clock in the morning to stoke the wood-burning stoves in each bathroom so that there would be hot water by the time the family awakened.

Jóska and I had our first argument in our Budapest apartment. I remember standing by the window with my back to the living room, having had my say and still fuming. Suddenly, I felt a trickle of ice-cold water flowing down my neck. Jóska, very calm, grinning, was pouring ice water on me from a very ugly sterling silver pitcher we had received as a wedding present.

"I knew this thing would be good for something," he remarked casually as he used his handkerchief to mop drops of water off the back of my suit, our freshly waxed floor, and the Persian rug.

"Here, Éva, pour some on me! Then, from now on, whenever we argue, let's just wave the pitcher at each other as a reminder."

What a funny man I married, I thought, and burst out laughing.

Jóska annoyed me from time to time, particularly when he came home late for dinner.

"Why are you late again?" I asked him one evening.

"None of your business," he replied in keeping with the male prerogative of the time to come and go as he pleased. For the next ten years, I never asked him again, and after a while he realized that his coming late did not improve dinner. I think he also became aware that I wasn't the least bit jealous or suspicious. One day he spontaneously told me where he had been—delayed at work for some reason. After that, he even started telephoning when he knew he would be late.

Contrary to custom, I too was completely free to do anything I wanted. Once Jóska went to Cservölgy for two days. The first night that he was gone, unbeknown to him, I went to the theater with my parents. Apu took Mother and me to a late supper afterward. When I entered the apartment at 1:30 in the morning I found Jóska asleep. I hadn't left a note since he wasn't due back until the next day. I didn't volunteer anything, to see if he'd ask me where I'd been, but he never did.

Jóska worked at the Agricultural Museum, where he had risen rapidly to the position of director. According to Hungarian custom, he had two months' vacation in the summer, which allowed him time to run the farm. As part of his job, he experimented with crops, which enabled him to make additional trips to Cservölgy.

I arranged and enjoyed our very active social life. I also spent many hours seated at our Steinway piano in the living room, pouring my happiness into the keyboard. I loved the glint of the setting sun on the rich mahogany piano top and tried to be home as often as I could to play at twilight. The parquet floors throughout the apartment forced the notes to rise, surrounding me with comfort and well-being.

The Nazi Nightmare

In the late 1930s, as Hitler's name became prominent in the minds of Europeans and as the horror of his deeds in Germany began to unfold, I started to give more thought to my Jewish ancestors. In Szekszárd, where I had spent the early years of my life, Jews who had converted to Catholicism, as my parents had done, had been accepted into the local society.

Most of my friends were children of the small-town Catholic elites—judges, attorneys, and county officials. During my school years, when my classmates and I occasionally made fun of the Jewish children, I never felt the derision applied to me. In fact, I gave it very little thought.

Later, I grew up in a secular, though mixed society in Budapest. After the 1919 interregnum, during which the Communists were in power and in which the Jews played a prominent part, there had been a wave of anti-Semitism directed at the Jews in civil service. Many of them were dismissed from their jobs. Those who had converted to Catholicism, however, were left alone.

I remember asking Jóska a few months before we were married whether his parents "hated Jews more than necessary"—the accepted criterion for Hungarian anti-Semitism. (Depending on the political winds, it often became prudent to pretend to hate Jews.)

"Only as much as necessary," he grinned and went on to tell me that his parents' favorite daughter-in-law-to-be (referring to me) would be the only one with Jewish heritage. As far as our marriage was concerned, the anti-Semitism did not seem to affect anything. Anyone married to a gentile became accepted anywhere.

One day in the spring of 1938, Jóska returned home from work and found me sitting in front of my dressing table, brushing my hair. He told me that an acquaintance of his, René Moulin, some kind of VIP whom I didn't recall meeting, had called and commented that Jóska shouldn't keep his wife under wraps. René had chided Jóska for not realizing that he was married to the most beautiful woman in Budapest.

Jóska looked into the mirror over my shoulder and examined me with care, as though thinking that one over. I glanced at my reflection and chuckled to myself. *Not bad for a mother of two,* I thought.

Just a few days before, a young soldier had climbed onto a streetcar behind me and, as I took a seat, had clicked his heels and said, "Excuse me, Ma'am, but I must tell you, you have the most beautiful legs in all of Budapest."

Jóska said that René had asked him to invite me to attend a new French conversation class, followed by a social hour at a casino that was, in fact, an old club for gentiles. I had been there once or twice, and Jóska went there regularly for stag parties. On the appointed day I picked my way through the slush on the roadway to the red brick mansion that housed the casino, careful not to get my taupe suede heels wet.

"*Madame, vous étes ravissante,*" Jóska's friend, a retired colonel, fawned on me as I entered.

I wore a peacock-blue suit under my fur stole and a matching pillbox hat, and spoke fluent French when I conversed with René. He pampered me with mint truffles and champagne.

During tea, Colonel Moulin remarked that they had problems with Jews at the casino.

"What problems?" asked one of the ladies. "We don't have Jewish members, do we?" I felt uneasy listening to her, but said nothing.

"No," said the colonel. "But some of the members have Jewish wives whom they keep trying to bring along to various functions, and there doesn't seem to be any way to stop them."

What a fool, I thought. I could see he had no idea about my ancestry.

When it was time to leave, the colonel rushed out to help me with my fur stole. He wanted to be absolutely sure that I would be coming again the following week.

"You just said you didn't want me here," I said, surprised at the words that came out of my mouth, never before having considered myself Jewish.

He turned quite pale and apologized profusely. "I had no idea," he stammered.

Annoyed, rather than angry or worried, I regarded this incident as stupid nonsense and more of an aggravation than anything else.

On the way home, though, I felt depressed. *Some people hate me just for the blood that runs through my veins,* I thought.

I told Jóska when I arrived home that I felt we had enough friends without going where I was not wanted.

"René is a pompous ass," Jóska said, and we left it at that.

I never went back to the casino.

Shortly after the incident at the French tea, we received a disturbing phone call from András.

"I heard from a good friend in Vienna that there have been widespread attacks on Jews and their property by the Nazi Party, both in Germany and Austria," he told us.

"How can civilized people like the Germans put up with this sort of goings-on?" Jóska asked, taking a step closer to me and putting his arm around my shoulder. I felt protected whatever might come our way.

"It certainly wouldn't be tolerated here," András replied.

I was not so sure but didn't contradict him, since I had no basis for my opinion, except for the silly incident at the casino.

During the fall of 1938, we learned of synagogues being set on fire and demolished throughout Germany and of thousands of Jews being arrested.

In spite of these events, our routine continued as before.

Since government offices closed at two in the afternoon, often Jóska returned home at that time. To me, when he appeared, it was as if the sun had risen all over again. Though we did ordinary things, our time together was somehow special. We had our midday dinner, and unless he needed to return to the office, he worked in the study of our apartment. He kept small toys on his desk for the children. Often these were fragile and needed frequent repairs. Sometimes he would confer with Livia and Ági in whispers, and then the three of them would leave the apartment.

"Where are you going?" I asked on one such occasion. "Going out," said the lead conspirator, grinning as he shut the door behind himself and two delighted little girls. They reappeared, sometime later, with telltale ice cream stains on the children's faces and blouses.

Sometimes he'd arrive home breathless, with plans for a quick run on a ski slope just outside Budapest. Or he'd urge me to grab my coat so we could go to a movie. On occasion, at the last minute, he'd decide we should all go to his parents' or my parents' home for dinner. Neither my mother nor my mother-in-law ever objected to anything Jóska did, though I'm sure both would have appreciated a phone call.

"Why are there hardly ever any cookies at our house?" he'd tease me. "My mother always has some." Of course, he knew very well that he had sneaked the last of our cookies to the children the night before.

Jóska was very pleased with our apartment. He loved the grand piano, the glistening parquet floors, and the fresh flowers I tried to keep on hand most of the year. His family, though of excellent pedigree, lived simply, with few trimmings. He and his six older siblings had been raised on his father's salary as a school superintendent, and they had money only for the bare necessities.

After World War II began in 1939, and victory after victory

for Germany followed, many Hungarians shifted their allegiance to the Germans. Perhaps they were positioning themselves in case of an invasion, or their loyalties were due to our close geographic proximity and family ties. Some of our friends who had changed their names years ago, even centuries before, to sound more Hungarian than German, took back their German names. We wondered whether Jewish persecution could come to pass in Hungary.

Jóska's family was wonderful to me even as the treatment of Jews went from bad to worse. They repeatedly told me that I must always remember that I belonged to their family—to try not to think about what was going on in Germany. Then they added the often heard phrase, "It can't happen here."

But it did. Hitler insisted on a right-of-way for his troops to cross Hungary on their way to the Russian front. Count Pál Teleki, then premier of Hungary, resisted to the last. He attempted to work out an agreement to keep Hungary neutral. When Hungary entered the war on the German side, he tried to conclude a separate armistice with the Western powers, but failed. In a dramatic protest against Nazi aggression, he shot himself. Much to our horror, the very next day the German army marched through Budapest.

In 1940, we heard that Szekszárd, my childhood hometown, had been designated as a reporting center for forced labor. All Jewish males under the age of forty-five were mobilized in an auxiliary unit, together with other Hungarian citizens whom the authorities would not allow to join the armed forces. Jews supervised the units, wearing white armbands on their sleeves.

Under Hungarian law, everyone had to register with the government. The registration information on file included not only current religious affiliation but lineage. Thus Jews could readily be identified and located.

From that time on, Jewish persecution began in earnest. At first, the spouses of gentiles were exempt, along with Catholic priests of Jewish descent, men with the highest military decorations, and other similar categories of Jews. The Nazis ordered all other Jews moved to ghetto houses and confiscated their possessions.

Though upset by these events, I still read newspaper accounts of them and listened to them discussed with a somewhat impersonal detachment. Though I was aware of my lineage, having been raised a Catholic, I did not regard myself as a Jew and convinced myself that no one else thought of me as one either.

We read in the newspaper that the Jewish unit from Szekszárd had been employed in paving roads near the town; then in the fall of 1942, we were dismayed to learn that the unit had been sent to the Ukrainian front where they were used as human mine detectors and perished.

My parents still had a home in Szekszárd in which they lived from time to time. In 1942, the Nazis confiscated the house along with all its contents. Apu and Mother received an official letter at their home in Budapest, instructing them to report to a ghetto house. They were to share their new home with six other families. German officers took over their house in Budapest.

We learned sometime later that those Jews who had not been conscripted into the labor unit from Szekszárd had been transported to a camp in Pécs, thence to Auschwitz. Luckily, my parents had been in Budapest, not at Szekszárd. Among those rounded up was my Aunt Böske—Mother's youngest sister, my cousin Stephen's mother—who died in the gas chambers there. *What would become of Stephen, who just the summer before had spent carefree weeks with us on the farm? For that matter, what would become of us all?*

When my parents received the order to report to one of the ghetto houses the Nazis had set up, I received a frantic call from my mother. "We have to leave the house in two hours. What should we do?"

It was perhaps the first time my mother had called me for

advice. "Your father is wandering around the house, just shaking his head."

"Don't waste time! Pack the warmest clothes you have. Winter is coming. Take medicines and any dried food. Take family photos. I'll try to bring you whatever else you need. I'll pick you up at four and drive you." I hesitated, "Tell Apu that I love you both."

As I hung up, I realized that I had never said those words to my mother before. The call had truly unnerved me. My hand shook as I hung up the telephone. What would happen to my parents? There were rumors of Jews being deported to Poland to labor camps. My parents could never stand up to hard physical work.

At four o'clock, I left Jóska in charge of the children and drove to my parents' home on Szomloi *út* (street) to pick them up. I felt a chill in the air as I walked through their garden. *Very different from the balmy day of our wedding,* I thought, as I unlocked the front door.

"Apu!" I exclaimed, shocked at the sight of my father standing in the foyer next to two large suitcases with a yellow Star of David on his gray winter coat. "Must you . . . .?" I never completed the question, as he nodded. I knew that all Jews had to wear one. I threw my arms around him.

"It's humiliating," he spoke quietly into my ear. As I let go of him, I looked up at his still handsome, sad face. It struck me that at sixty-five, with blue eyes and his light brown hair graying at the temples, he appeared Aryan, not at all what we thought of as Jewish— dark Middle Eastern.

Mother came down the stairs carrying a hat box, as though bound for London on one of her trips. I held my tongue. Our normally cool relationship yielded to the apprehension of the moment as she hugged me.

"They said Borcsa *néni* can't come with us. I've let her go to stay with her family," Mother said, reaching up to smooth her hair, an indication of her anxiety. Borcsa *néni* had been living at my parents' when we were not at Cservölgy.

"We have to share a bathroom with fifteen other people," Apu added with indignation.

In spite of the circumstances, I smiled inwardly. "That should be the least of your worries," I told him, but it shocked me that both my parents appeared old and looked to me for guidance.

When I later mentioned this conversation to Jóska, he laughed. "Well, perhaps it's time your father learned how to run his own bathwater." Jóska referred to the standing joke in the family that my father pretended not to know how to run his bath, and would ring for a servant to do it for him.

I loaded my parents' suitcases in the trunk with Apu's help. He and Mother climbed in the back seat, she holding the hatbox on her lap. I sat in the driver's seat and started the engine. A car with swastikas on the doors pulled up just as we drove from the house. Through the rearview mirror, I watched as three men in black uniforms, with red swastikas on their armbands, bounded out of the car toward my parents' front gate. I made an abrupt turn at the nearest corner to block out the sight, in the hope that my parents had not seen the men. I don't think they did since they made no comment.

The apartment house, on a side street near the Danube, to which Mother and Apu had been assigned bore a giant Star of David over the front door. It had been designated a ghetto house. Rules were posted on a sheet of paper emblazoned with swastikas that bore the letterhead of the Hungarian Nazi Party. In addition to regulations governing shared cooking and bathroom arrangements, permission to leave the building was limited to two-hour periods on Tuesday and Thursday afternoons, with only one family member allowed out at any time.

The odor of cooked cabbage permeated the stairway as we dragged my parents' belongings up to the third floor, then made our way through a group of youngsters who were playing in a cramped corridor. The door to one apartment stood open. A young woman seemed to be keeping an eye on the children.

"Please, Éva, just leave us now and go home," Apu pleaded as we dropped the suitcases at the door to the unit he and Mother were to share with two other families.

I protested, but Apu was adamant.

"Promise you'll stay away from here," he begged me. "For the sake of the girls," he warned.

Even at this point my own safety had not concerned me. After all, I had been baptized Catholic as an infant, and the Nazi directives governing the lives of Jews did not apply to me. My parents' circumstances were different because they had converted to Catholicism as adults. None of us was particularly religious. Jóska, the children, and I attended Catholic services, mostly at Christmas and Easter, as was the custom among many Hungarians.

I could see, though, even if I wasn't concerned, that Apu was worried about my safety, so I kissed my parents good-bye. "I'll meet you Tuesday on the riverbank by the bridge," I told Mother, "and bring you some groceries."

As I made my way back to the street, the children we'd seen playing in the corridor had disappeared inside their apartment and the sound of a melancholy tune floated from under their door. *What would happen to my parents? What dreadful times these were,* I thought.

Uneasy weeks followed. One or another of our workers still periodically made the perilous journey from Cervölgy to our apartment in Budapest. Along with news of the farm, they would bring us fresh produce, which had become unavailable under the recently imposed rationing system. Supplies were randomly confiscated at checkpoints. I delivered some of the food from the farm to Mother on Tuesdays and exchanged confidences, she complaining about their circumstances, and I telling her about the children. Then on Thursdays Apu and I would meet at a bakery near their apartment, trading scary rumors about the war and the Jewish situation.

Each day, empty train cars stood at the ready at the Keleti Railway Station. Two or three transports had already left for camps in Poland.

"When I asked him why they were sending Jews to Poland, one of the security men at our building let slip something about a 'final solution,'" Apu confided at one of our meetings.

"I pressed him for more information, but he backtracked and said the people were needed to work in the war effort. They can't expect Mother and me to do heavy work, can they?" he asked me, anxiety written on his face.

At that moment, two SS men entered the bakery. All conversation ceased. The baker, standing behind the counter, turned pale. Once they had walked past where we were sitting, I kissed Apu and slipped out the door to the street, while the officers approached the counter. I stood in a doorway, out of sight, until Apu emerged from the shop, and surreptitiously followed him back to his apartment to make sure he was safe. Then, as darkness descended, I headed for home.

Weeks went by, with rumors increasing and apprehension rising.

In June 1944, over BBC Radio, came the news that the Allies had landed in Normandy. Once the Americans began their advance through France, no one in his right mind, not even the Arrow Cross (the Hungarian Nazi Party) members, doubted for a moment that the outcome would be victory for the Allies. The high regard in which America was held in Hungary led us to believe that the side helped by the United States could not lose a war. But how long would it take until their victory, and what would happen to us in the meantime?

In anticipation that the Germans might want to resolve the fate of the Jews before the end came, we decided it would be advisable for me to get false documents. I had been using my civil service ID to which I was entitled as Jóska's wife. However, the Nazis at checkpoints all over town asked for proof of lineage and religion as well as identification. The bridges over the Danube had been mined at the direction of the German High Command, so I made the trip to Pest in a small ferryboat. I went to a place where such documents were sold by Transylvanian refugees. My father had learned of the agency from a friend he met while standing in line at the butcher shop. I paid dearly for a counterfeit birth certificate, identity card, and driver's license. On the birth certificate my lineage appeared to be Christian back to my great-great-grandparents.

I hurriedly left the building after obtaining the documents. I walked several blocks before I dared to stop. Shielded by the trunk of a chestnut tree from people scurrying in and out of neighborhood shops, I stuffed the papers into my purse. The afternoon sun filtered through the budding branches, heralding the coming of summer. A lorry loaded with German soldiers drove past, honking its way through sparse traffic. I felt as though they were coming for me. I expected the truck to screech to a halt, and that the whole truckload of troops would descend on me to inspect my purse. I forced myself to walk at a normal pace toward the river. Several German staff cars and motorcycles with sidecars passed me, but no one gave me a second glance. On the ferry crossing the Danube, I tried my best to look nonchalant while sitting on one of the benches on deck. My stomach churned, knowing the papers might be inspected when the boat reached the other side of the river. My heart pounded so hard when we docked, I was sure everyone around me could hear. As we disembarked, a burly thug, standing at the head of the gangplank, asked for religious identification. My hands shook as I gave the papers to the black-uniformed man. His shirt bore the emblem of the Arrow Cross. He leered at me for a moment, glanced at my documents, and waved me through.

Empty trains still stood at the Budapest railroad station. No one knew why. Trainloads of Jews were leaving the countryside daily, and horror stories of the camps at Auschwitz and elsewhere kept circulating.

We attempted to keep up routines for the sake of the children, sending them to school, shopping for food, and even visiting friends. Most of our days were spent trying to help my parents and other relatives. As we took food to the ghetto houses, we also passed on information about Jewish relatives. By then, everybody with any decency at all was horrified by the situation, and especially people such as us, in a mixed marriage, tried to do what we could to help others, although it was extremely dangerous to do so. There were daily reports of people being informed upon, sometimes by family members.

A few days after having secured the false identity papers, on my way home for lunch, I bought a newspaper down by the Chain Bridge. I sat on a bench to peruse the front page. "Jewish Exemptions Repealed," read the headline over the right hand column. All the exemptions to the Jewish regulations (such as being married to a Christian) had been canceled. From that day the various laws governing Jewish life would apply to all except persons married to priests and military officers with the highest decorations. Therefore, they would apply to me. The false papers I had acquired might clear me through a checkpoint, but they would never withstand serious scrutiny.

I rose from the bench. I still remember that a light wind was blowing and that there were billowing, white clouds overhead, as I stood for a moment with a sinking feeling before starting up the hill toward home.

Jóska burst in the front door minutes after I reached our apartment. His presence always reassured me.

"I came as soon as I heard," he said. "I waited half an hour for the streetcar in front of the museum," he continued, breathless from having dashed up the hill from the Chain Bridge stop.

"What do you think I should do? Go into hiding somewhere? Go to Cservölgy? What?"

"Slow down a minute," Jóska interrupted me. "We must think this through very carefully." He took me by the hand. Sunlight filtered through the sheer white curtains and bounced off the polished mahogany of the piano, lending the living room an air of peace, at odds with the turmoil I felt.

"Where are the children?" Jóska asked, as he led me toward the couch.

"Bebe picked them up from school for me," I replied. "She'll bring them home after supper.

"What do you think I should do, Jóska?" I repeated. In my mind I kept turning over various scenarios.

"It will take the Nazis time to implement the new rules," Jóska said to reassure me.

"But what if the knock on the door comes tonight? What if a notice comes in the mail to report somewhere? Should I try to get to Cservölgy, do you think?" I repeated.

"Two more days until the school year ends," my husband reminded me. "I think it's worth the risk waiting until then to go as a family. You are less likely to arouse suspicion than if you go by yourself."

"Remember the day we were married by the registrar? What you said about divorce? Don't feel you have to stand by me to be chivalrous," I reminded Jóska.

"We could get a divorce and just live together for the safety of the children," he replied.

"That I'm not willing to do, Jóska. The girls are ten and seven, old enough to know what's going on, and I don't want to scandalize them."

"You are worrying about appearances at a time like this?" Jóska exclaimed.

"It matters to me," I said. "If harm could come to any of you because of me, I'll just leave. Perhaps I could try for the border."

We left it at that for the moment. I suppose there would have been maybe a one percent chance of getting across the border into Yugoslavia or Italy.

At that time Jóska still had his job, although he had not been promoted to the next civil service grade because of being married to me. Advancements had been suspended in such cases. Official records showed my lineage, not just my Catholic religion. Jóska having a wife with Jewish ancestry had become a huge liability.

A few days later, over the radio came a new twist to the recently promulgated laws. The Jewish wives of gentiles with children, married before 1930, were exempt. Jóska and I had been married in 1928. We heard later that this particular wrinkle in the regulations was tailored to fit one of the Nazi big shots, who had a Jewish wife. This applied to women only. If a husband was Jewish, married to a gentile, he would be deported. So, by an incredible stroke of luck, I was home free once again, for the moment at least.

We listened to the broadcast during dinner. I started shaking. Jóska, silently—in order not to alarm the girls—brought me some brandy. The dining room light glinted off his signet ring as he handed the glass to me. It reminded me of the disparity of our lineage—his ancient Hungarian, mine Jewish—leaving me feeling alone and very vulnerable.

The Boot

As the next few months passed, laws governing the Jews changed almost daily. At checkpoints, the Nazis yanked Jews out of line. Deportation notices appeared on the walls of houses where Jews lived. As more and more Jews disappeared, fear for my parents and for myself became a part of my daily life. Every stranger who passed portended possible arrest.

One afternoon during this time of living in the shadows, my cousin Peter rang our doorbell, nervously glancing over his shoulder. He and I had not been particularly close, so I wondered what on earth he was doing at our apartment.

His branch of the family had not converted to Catholicism. As a result, he had recently been arrested, moved to a ghetto house, and assigned to hard labor. Here he stood on our doorstep, not wearing his Star of David as regulations required, apparently absent without leave from the work detail.

He looked gaunt, disheveled, and dirty, his black, curly hair tangled. He had dark circles under his eyes.

I found myself feeling sorry for Peter. I was glad Jóska wasn't home for he would have been very angry. My cousin exposed us to great risk by coming to our house.

I invited him in, and he told me about his escape from a roadwork crew. As we spoke, he kept glancing out the window, checking the square in front of the house.

"I know a man named Yoshi, a chauffeur at the Japanese embassy," he told me.

"Where on earth did you meet him?" I asked.

"Never mind that now," Peter replied, irritated by my interruption. "Yoshi promised to drive me across the border into Austria, in a car with diplomatic plates. He said those are never searched."

Though Yoshi's plan sounded too good to be true, I said

nothing to dissuade Peter. These were desperate days. Profiteers were taking great risks for the right price, so perhaps Peter had to take the chance.

"I gave some money to my friend Maria, for safekeeping. I want you to get it. She works at the papal legation," Peter blurted out.

The legation housed the home and offices of the papal nuncio, the pope's representative to the Hungarian government. The compound happened to be located across Disz *tér*, the square in front of our house.

"Please, Éva, go and get it for me...Now!"

"Peter, for God's sake, look out the window again."

Jews, who for various reasons had not yet been detained, were lined up on the other side of the square, waiting to pick up some sort of exemption document available at the legation. The papal delegate, like many of the clergy, tried with limited success to save lives.

The legation loomed like a dark fortress under an overcast winter sky. The seventeenth-century building combined Baroque and Roman architecture to present an impressive facade. It had tall, arched windows and bold ornamentation over a massive, highly polished, wooden door. So far, the building had remained intact.

"How in the world do you expect me to get in there, Peter?"

"My life is at stake," he replied.

Never mind mine, I thought—but said nothing. I was glad that Jóska wasn't home to stop me. I sometimes thought he worried about my safety more than I did.

I left Peter in charge of the girls, who were playing in their room, grabbed my winter coat, and went out into the gray, dreary afternoon. With trepidation, I walked over to the front door of the legation, bypassing the long line of people waiting to enter.

Without even looking at me, the Arrow Cross guard at the door shouted, "Go back to the end of the line."

"Can't you see I'm not Jewish?" I said, managing to sound

very angry. I pulled out my government identification card. Now it was the guard's turn to be alarmed. Jóska was director of the Agricultural Museum, but I might have been the wife of some big shot for all he knew.

"Please forgive me, ma'am, I am very sorry."

I inclined my head with suitable *hauteur* and walked into the legation. An old nun in a voluminous black habit sat inside the door and directed me to Maria's office.

"I am Peter Gundig's cousin," I said, approaching the young woman sitting behind a desk. Maria appeared excessively thin, rather tall, and frail. She observed me with a suspicious gaze.

"He sent me to pick up the funds he left with you."

"Wait here," Maria said, rising to leave the room, shutting the door behind her. I felt too nervous to sit down. I paced up and down her small office. The room contained only a desk, a filing cabinet, and two chairs. Interminable minutes passed, and I wondered where Maria had gone. I didn't want to be away from the apartment too long. I glanced around the sparsely furnished office, and my eyes rested on a wall plaque.

"To Maria Fekete with appreciation for her work with Boy Scout Troop 94," it said. Jóska had mentioned that some Scouts spied on their families for the Nazis.

Maria had been gone for several minutes, and I felt alarmed. *What could be taking so long? Perhaps I should leave.* I opened the door to the corridor, and as I did so Maria reappeared. She handed me an envelope and gave a nervous smile, filling me with unease. "Count it," she said, in a throaty voice.

"I'm sure it's all here," I replied, anxious to go. "Peter will be most grateful. Goodbye, Maria." I took the envelope from her and left.

The Nazi guard came to attention as I passed him on my way out.

I felt elated that I had accomplished my mission without

incident. The sun had come out while I had been inside and warmed me. I fingered the envelope in my pocket and glanced at the line of people waiting to enter the legation. Anxiety was etched on every face. I tightened my grip on the envelope containing Peter's money.

As I was about to cross the square to our apartment, a staff car bearing SS insignia screeched to a halt, blocking my path. *Oberlieutenant* Weiss, whom I immediately recognized from newspaper pictures as being the German officer in charge of hunting down escaping Jews, bolted from the car and blocked my path. The lieutenant had a reputation for playing cat-and-mouse with Jews. He was known to enjoy terrorizing people.

"*Gnädige Frau*" (honored lady), he said, using the respectful German form of address in derision. He raised his right hand to his temple in a mocking gesture of salute. As the hand descended, I noticed his mouth was quite misshapen. A badly botched cleft palate, perhaps. "I am given to understand that you are carrying some funds for your cousin Peter." Weiss glared at me, glancing at the envelope I clutched in my hand as he said this.

My heart sank, as I tried to keep all expression from my face. *How could he know this? Had Maria at the legation betrayed Peter? Had someone followed Peter to our apartment? What would happen to me? What would happen to the children? Why had I done this?* I glanced involuntarily at our apartment windows.

"There must be some mistake, *Herr Oberlieutenant*," I answered, trying to appear calm. "Peter is at the Chain Bridge House, and you know no one is allowed in there."

A sharp bark emanating from inside the lieutenant's car diverted my attention. A Doberman's head and paws appeared in the rear-door window.

"Don't trifle with me. You know as well as I do that Peter is at your apartment with the children," the lieutenant responded, ignoring the dog.

I hoped my winter coat would keep him from seeing that I

was shaking. Did he really know or was he bluffing? I became aware that the Jews standing in line waiting to enter the legation were staring at me.

Help me, I thought, inwardly screaming. *Somebody help me!*

The dog barked again, and the lieutenant reached over and opened the car door. The Doberman leaped from the staff car to the sidewalk and crouched near the curb to defecate a few feet in front of me. The lieutenant observed this with nonchalance and before I could think of what to say next, he extended his mirror-polished black boot and stepped into the excrement. For the life of me I couldn't figure out what he was doing. He turned to me with hatred in his eyes.

"I will make you a bargain, *Gnädige Frau,*" he said, extending his boot in my direction.

"You lick the sole of my boot clean and you will see your children again. We will forget about our little conversation. If not," he said with a glance at the Doberman, "my friend is hungry."

Time went into slow motion. I saw the girls being torn apart by that Doberman. I saw Jóska trying to intervene and being shot. I saw my head under the lieutenant's heel, being crushed into the excrement. I was aware of the line of Jews frozen in their tracks. *Why doesn't somebody help me? Don't they know that it will be their turn next? Catholics would help,* I thought illogically, perhaps remembering Jóska's often-expressed family loyalty to me. I felt a dread of things to come, and revulsion to my innermost being, at what I knew I must do.

The moment passed as a shroud of depression and horror enveloped me. I sank to my knees in the snow and closed my eyes. As I licked the feces from his boot, my throat and stomach convulsed and I gathered all my will to keep from vomiting.

I tried to stand up.

"Clean, please," came the command.

I opened my eyes and saw a worm move in the excrement, as the lieutenant moved his foot ever so slightly upward, pushing the feces-coated worm into my nose. I gagged and convulsed. The Doberman's fangs were close to my face, and I could feel his hot breath. Then, as though my mind could not endure what I must do, I was aware of licking the boot, but felt nothing. I just kept licking, for what seemed like an eternity, until suddenly the lieutenant jerked his foot, kicking me hard in the chest. I fell backward in the snow. In pain, hardly able to breathe, I held back my tears.

Glancing up at the children's window across the square, I thought I saw the curtains move. God, I hoped the children hadn't seen any of this.

Without a word, the lieutenant turned. He gave a sharp command to the Doberman, which bounded into the staff car. Lieutenant Weiss followed with a command to the driver and was gone.

I retched in the snow for a long time. A lone woman stepped from the line of waiting Jews and without a word handed me a handkerchief before blending back into the crowd. I wiped my mouth as best I could, staggered to my feet, crossed the square, and went home. To my relief, the children were intent on a game of checkers when I entered the apartment.

Peter came rushing to the door.

"Did you get it?" he asked.

I handed him the envelope. I could not bring myself to ask him whether he had seen what had happened. Peter had been playing with the children and gave no hint that he had seen anything.

I vowed never to tell anyone, not even Jóska, for I was so ashamed of what I had been forced to do.

"I'll never forget this, Éva," Peter said, looking me in the eye.

He stepped toward me to give me a kiss. I turned my head, so he wouldn't smell the feces and the vomit on my breath. His lips brushed my cheek and he left.

The War Rolls On

Before my encounter with the lieutenant, both my parents had become ill with severe colds. I delivered provisions to them at the ghetto house, rather than meeting them in public.

My confrontation with Lieutenant Weiss left me numb and terrified. The day after, I waited until nightfall to visit my parents. Working my way through the shadows, avoiding streetlights, I approached their building. From across the street, I could see the flicker of a cigarette lighter in the entryway. I flattened myself against a wall and held my breath. *What if the Germans had posted sentries? Had the man seen me? How would I get the food past him? How could I get away?* Questions raced through my mind as I eyed the flame. Then, when it connected with the tip of a cigarette, the light illuminated Apu's face. I let out my breath and ran across the street.

"Thank God it's you!" I whispered as I hugged him. "I thought you were a guard. Since when do you smoke?" I added.

"No one who doesn't live here is allowed inside anymore," he informed me, ignoring my question about his smoking. "Best you go at once." Apu relieved me of the shopping bag I had been carrying. We exchanged family news for a couple of minutes, and then I slunk back into the darkness and headed home.

Steven Molnár, a high-ranking Hungarian army officer whom I met after the war, once went to one of the ghetto houses in full uniform. He told the guards that he had orders to transport two people to another camp. He gave the names of two Jews he knew slightly. The ruse worked, and the women's lives were saved. I remember asking him why on earth he had done it—risking his own neck for near strangers—considering that he claimed to dislike Jews.

"I did it as a lark," he said.

I didn't quite believe him. I felt that because Steven was a decent man from a good Hungarian family, he could not have stood by, watching what was going on without trying to help.

In June every year, Jóska and I would take the children and go to Cservölgy to oversee the fruit harvest. I made arrangements with Alice Mercer, who had hired Apu to work for the Red Cross during World War I, to help my parents once again and keep them supplied with necessities. Alice, although a British citizen, had chosen to remain in Budapest in spite of the war. "My heart is Hungarian," she had said when I asked why she hadn't left the country.

With an uneasy feeling, we made the trip to Cservölgy for the summer of 1944.

As the Allies advanced, the brutality of the Nazis increased. Eighteen of our relatives, among them my father's elderly sister Luisa and her sick husband, were deported, herded, and packed into cattle cars, standing for days on their way to Auschwitz and the gas chambers.

The previous fall, Peter had given us some of his mother's jewels and stock certificates and asked us to hide them at the farm. We walled up the jewels inside the house. Jóska wanted to hide the papers in a hollow tree he knew of in the forest. He asked me to come with him and carry a rifle, so that if somebody came I could fire into the air to alert him. I thought we shouldn't try to hide the documents on a Sunday, that being the day on which the farm workers were likely to go into the woods looking for mushrooms. But Jóska insisted. I think our nerves were in bad shape by then and he wasn't thinking clearly. If anyone saw us and reported our activities directly or gossiped about them in the village, word would reach the authorities and we could be executed for aiding Jews.

"If you are afraid, stay home," I remember him saying.

I was afraid, but of course I wouldn't stay home. Sure enough, while he was hiding the papers, I heard rustling coming from the bushes to my left. I peered in that direction, trying to see what caused the noise. The rustling stopped. Maybe it was a forest creature. Then to my horror, I spotted the familiar figure of Gombász *bácsi* (a term of affection and respect), one of the local mushroom pickers bent at his task. He was too close for me to try to warn Jóska.

Concealed by a bush, I raised the rifle Jóska had handed to me when he had posted me on sentry duty, and zeroed the sight on Gombász *bácsi*'s forehead. I could feel sweat pouring down my spine. My hands shook. I looked at the harshly scored face of the old man I had known for years and knew I couldn't pull the trigger. I lowered the rifle. Gombász *bácsi* made no indication that he'd seen me and poked along, stirring leaves with a stick, hunting for mushrooms. The next night there was a confidential message from the village police that we had better leave; they had a search warrant issued by the Nazis. Perhaps the old man had seen us after all.

So we packed up the children, took what food we could gather, and went by train to Budapest.

A few weeks later in the fall of 1944, just before the siege of Budapest began, we received another message from the police at Totvázsony, letting us know that it was all right to come back to Cservölgy. The whole matter had blown over.

By then it was too late; Budapest had been cut off from the farm by the advancing Russian army, and we could not have returned to Cservölgy even if we had wanted to do so.

The Germans had great respect for art, architecture, and historic monuments. Since Budapest had many sixteenth-century buildings constructed during the time of the Turkish occupation, conventional wisdom at the time had us believe that the Germans would surrender Budapest rather than destroy the city. We always thought that when the time came, Budapest would be declared an "open city," allowing the conquering armies to advance without a fight. It didn't occur to us that the Germans would defend Budapest just to gain a few more days in power.

On September 2, when Jóska, the children, and I arrived at our apartment in the city, periodic air raids had begun. Mr. Denk, who lived in the apartment next door to us, came out into the hallway when he heard the elevator door clang shut. "I'm surprised you came back to the city," he greeted Jóska and me, and smiled at the girls. "My wife and I are returning to Munich, where my family came from fifty years ago."

"Don't you think Budapest will be declared an open city?" Jóska asked him.

"I heard on the BBC that Buda at least, along with Vienna, may be spared," I chimed in.

"But the industrial parts of Pest have already been hit twice," Mr. Denk responded. "We're not waiting for them to make a mistake. I'll give you a key to our apartment before we leave."

Jóska turned to unlock our front door. Many people, it seemed, were moving to Austria and Germany, fleeing the advancing Russian army.

That night, within seconds of an air raid siren waking us, we saw a flash around the edges of our blackout shades, felt the building shake with a blast, and heard glass breaking. I leaped out of bed to go to the children. As I ran through the living room, which separated our bedroom from theirs, broken glass crunched under my slippers.

I threw open the door to Livia and Ági's room and, to my relief, saw that they were both fast asleep.

"Leave it to those two to miss all the excitement," Jóska said, standing behind me, just as a second, more distant explosion rattled the shutters. Jóska flipped on the living room lights, and we could see shards sticking out of the window frames and broken glass on the parquet floor.

"So much for saving architectural treasures," I remarked. Though we lived just a few blocks from the beautiful Baroque royal palace, it seemed that we were not to be spared.

Looking through one of the broken front windows, we could see commotion in front of the war ministry, across the square. "That must have been the target," Jóska surmised. *This is what it feels like to be bombed*, I thought, surprised at my calm.

"Let's deal with the broken glass in the morning," Jóska suggested and headed back toward our bedroom. He managed to return to sleep within minutes.

I, on the other hand, in spite of taking sleeping pills, tossed and turned the rest of the night, weighing all our circumstances. The war had arrived at our doorstep. *If the Germans felt they were running out of time, would they intensify their roundup of Jews? Should we have stayed on the farm? Would we survive?*

Next morning, after calming the children's excitement over the broken windows, we hustled them off to school. Jóska hoped he could find someone to make the necessary repairs.

Before he left for work, we renewed our debate begun the previous spring, whether or not we should divorce. This time it was Jóska who said we should stay together no matter what.

"What if I get a summons to report to the train station?" I asked him.

"Perhaps we should move to the museum," he replied, "so the notice wouldn't reach you."

"You know we can't move without registering the new address with the police," I said. Lifelong habits of obedience to the law were hard to shake.

Aside from the problem of my Jewish ancestors, we had endless theories about where it would be safest as the actual fighting approached Budapest.

"Do you think Pest would be safer?" I asked.

"All the industrial plants are over there," Jóska replied.

"Yes," I said, "but the royal palace and the military headquarters are on our side of the river."

"I've heard of people moving from Buda to Pest and others going in the opposite direction," Jóska responded. "There's no knowing what would be best."

Once again the discussion led nowhere, and we stayed in our apartment on the Buda side and awaited developments.

Since all the railroads were being used to carry war materials to the front, no glass could be found for the windows. Jóska brought home pieces of plywood, which we nailed to the window frames as best we could.

A few days after we had returned to the city in September, a young girl from Cservölgy joined us to help me with the housework. Katinka was the daughter of one of the farmhands. She had barely settled in when the air raids became frequent and severe; we sent her back home just before the Russian advance cut off access to the farm.

Then we heard a radio broadcast that I had expected all along. The exemptions had been lifted, and all Jewish women, such as myself, were ordered to be at a sports arena in the suburbs at ten the next morning.

The cloud of hatred that had enveloped me since the boot incident swirled ever closer around me. My immediate reaction to the announcement was fear, but it subsided rather rapidly as the need for planning for survival took over. The blind hatred that was directed at me for reasons totally beyond my control brought with it a lasting, deep depression.

From the day of the boot, I have never experienced pure joy or really even temporary happiness. When that incident took place, something snapped in the very core of my being, never to return. I could not bring myself to tell Jóska. I was afraid of what he might do in an attempt to retaliate against the lieutenant. On the other hand, I was perhaps a little bit afraid that even he might do nothing. From that day forward, there has always been in my life a twinge of doubt overshadowing all human contacts and, in the background, that ominous cloud of depression, ready to smother and destroy me.

A red leaf blew in through one of the partially boarded windows, reminding me that it was fall, my favorite season. It settled on the Persian carpet. I noticed it as I crossed the living room. I heard the mail being pushed through the slot in the front hall. The first envelope chased away all thoughts of a beautiful autumn day. I held in my hand a notice ordering me to report to the sports arena mentioned in the radio broadcast.

Jóska rushed home from work when he heard the noon news on the radio stating that summonses had been received all over the city. He threw his arms around me when I met him at the door and sat me down in the living room so that we could try to decide what I should do. He put his hand over mine, and once again I glanced at his signet ring, setting him apart from my Jewish ancestry.

"First of all," Jóska said, "you are not reporting to any sports stadium."

He said this with such finality that I felt the issue wasn't even open for discussion. I was overwhelmed with love for him. He had a way of making me feel secure, even under the worst of circumstances.

His statement confirmed my instinct to go into hiding and under no circumstances to capitulate to the order.

"I have to leave the house, Jóska. The building manager or someone else may be aware of my predicament and turn me in, or the Nazis may come for me. What am I to do?"

"Remember Adam's offer?" Jóska asked, referring to a young bachelor, a distant relative of his, who had a cottage somewhere in the Buda hills and had previously offered to let me stay there if it became necessary. He had promised he would bring me food.

"I remember. Could you try to reach him?" I asked.

Jóska dialed the number and while he waited for Adam to answer, I went to my room to put some essentials into a shopping bag. Jóska hung up just as I stepped back into the living room.

"Adam was killed in an air raid," he stated, relaying what Adam's housekeeper had told him. Jóska turned pale and looked worried. I sat down next to him, as shocked by the news as he.

On the piano stood a beautiful Italian cut-glass vase with a pale pink hyacinth I had splurged on at a flower stand. I remember the fragrance. It struck me how incongruous the vase and the flower looked with death and destruction all around us.

"We have to come up with some other solution. What will you do with the children if I find a place to hide?" I asked.

"I'll take a leave of absence and stay home with them."

The constant air raids made it almost impossible to get back and forth to his job anyway. He had endless German checkpoints to traverse.

I knew Jóska's suggestion was the right thing to do.

"What should we tell the girls?" I asked.

"Let's say you caught a ride to Cservölgy and went to pick up some food and will be back as soon as you can."

"Do you think I should wake Livia and Ági to say good-bye? I may never see them again."

"Best not do that. You may have trouble controlling your emotions and they would suspect something. Why worry them?"

"You're right," I told him, cracking the door to their room and peeking at their slumbering faces. I quietly shut the door without good-byes.

Jóska walked over to Laci and Bebe's house, close by, to see if our friends could come up with any ideas on where I could hide. Bebe's circumstances were similar to that of our children, however with a Jewish father and a gentile mother. Laci belonged to an old Hungarian family like Jóska. They were ready to help us in any way they could.

Laci suggested the papal legation as a place where he had heard that Jews were being sheltered.

The papal nuncio, as the pope's personal representative to the Hungarian government, lived and worked there, surrounded by church dignitaries. As such, he and the entire legation compound enjoyed diplomatic immunity. Our German occupiers, up until that time, had respected diplomatic regulations and regarded the compound as Vatican territory on which they did not impinge.

Jóska was not particularly religious and had ignored the legation for all the years during which we had lived in close proximity to it. He and Laci speculated that the compound would be unlikely to be searched since the Germans would not want to antagonize the pope, who had chosen largely to ignore Germany's anti-Jewish activities.

"Laci came up with a good idea," Jóska announced when he came home. "He thinks Jews are being sheltered at the papal legation across the square. Maybe they'd take you in."

I gasped, reminded of my encounter with Lieutenant Weiss, though Jóska didn't seem to notice my distress.

"I'd like to know what you think." Jóska looked at me, waiting for an answer. I still couldn't bring myself to tell him I had recently been there to retrieve Peter's money.

"Don't you suppose they are packed with people by now?" I asked.

"I'll go over right away. Maybe your cousin Peter's friend, Maria, can help you." Jóska was out the door again before I could say anything. I was terrified that it had been Maria who had informed on me when I'd picked up Peter's money. She might do so again.

Jóska returned a short time later. "Maria arranged an immediate interview for you with the nuncio himself for this evening and said to tell you to come, prepared to stay." Jóska looked visibly relieved.

I had hoped never to set foot at the legation again, but of course Jóska had no idea that I didn't want to go there. My evening appointment with the nuncio at least gave me time to be with the children for a few more hours.

At supper, I told Livia and Ági that I was going to Cservölgy for a few days, and that I would bring back some food.

"See if the chestnuts are ready to be picked yet," Livia suggested.

"Yes, and bring back some cheese," Ági instructed.

With a heavy heart, I promised to do what I could. I read them a story and put them to bed.

Since people in the neighborhood often carried canvas shopping bags, I chose that, instead of a suitcase, to pack a few essentials and waited until evening to hug Jóska good-bye. I clung to him until he gently pushed me away and opened the door.

"Remember, you'll just be across the square," he reminded me. "I'll walk the children by when I pick them up from school, so you can see them."

I carried my bag down the stairs, rather than riding the elevator, trying to prolong the time it took to reach the street.

A few days previously the Germans had set up a camouflaged infantry encampment in the square that I had to traverse to reach the papal legation. When I opened our front door and slipped out furtively into the chill wind, I could hear pots and pans clanging. No one was in sight, but a strong smell of cooked cabbage hung in the winter air. I had to pass the open flap of the German mess tent. As I approached the opening, a splash of water hit the ground in front of me. It splattered on my coat, and I jumped. A young soldier holding a bucket, who looked about fifteen, poked his head out of the tent. *They are drafting babies now,* I thought.

"*Entschuldigen sie mich,*" (Excuse me) the boy apologized.

"*Macht nichts,*" (It doesn't matter) I replied and hurried on. I forced myself to walk at a measured pace, past the spot where I had knelt to lick the lieutenant's boot. My humiliation haunted me. I did not know whether the nuncio would take me in or what would become of me.

I reached the legation door without further incident and

knocked. An icy wind whipped around me and I shivered, waiting to be admitted. The door cracked open after a few minutes and I stepped inside.

"Do come in, please. We are expecting you," said a smiling young priest who introduced himself as Father Matthew.

Relieved, I walked into a different world. The foyer, dimly lit by small candles, lay just inside the massive door.

"When the building next door was hit, our power went out," Father Matthew explained.

Children were playing marbles in the entryway.

The office, whence I had picked up Peter's money, loomed dark. There was no sign of Maria. Beyond it, through an archway, I could see a well-lit area with many candles illuminating a large room. As the priest led me through a hallway, it became evident that Jóska was not the first person to have thought of the legation as a hiding place. People familiar from the neighborhood peered out of doorways. To my surprise, one of them was the baker in whose shop Apu and I had been meeting. He nodded in recognition. I hadn't known he was a Jew. I was strangely comforted by his familiar presence. I could hear the BBC broadcast of the evening news coming from a radio in his room.

Maria had told Jóska that I should ask for His Excellency.

"His Excellency, Angelo Rotta, will see you in a few minutes," Father Matthew informed me. He led me upstairs into a room lined with books. Soon the nuncio came in. At age eighty, he carried the weight of the world on his shoulders, trying to do what little he could to save people. Although he was Italian, he spoke French, so I tried to say a few words of thanks. With a medieval gesture, he laid his right hand on my head.

"*Nos portes sont toujours ouvertes*" (Our doors are always open), he said gently.

I felt strange and safe in his presence. He did not consider me a refugee—not even a guest. Seemingly, I had found a home. Home, not just for me, but for perhaps fifty or sixty others, hiding from the terror that lurked on the far side of the ornate doorway through which I had entered a few moments before.

The door was manned after dark by various residents, who kept watch through a side window for visitors wishing to enter. Jóska would come over most evenings for a quick, furtive visit. We stood and talked quietly inside the entryway to try to have a bit of privacy.

Jóska managed somehow to take care of Livia and Ági, though he had never before had to act as mother and father to our children.

Bebe went to our apartment in the evenings to help give the girls their baths and put them to bed.

One afternoon, I waited near a window, keeping out of sight of the street, for Jóska to pass by with the children. They walked along on the sidewalk right in front of me. It warmed me that the girls wore their navy coats and matching red berets, which I had knitted for them. I could hear Jóska telling them to stop. He said something and handed a piece of chalk to Livia. She bent down and drew hopscotch lines on the pavement. There, almost close enough for me to touch them, she and Ági skipped and played. I could hear Jóska laugh when one of the girls lost her balance and staggered in an exaggerated attempt not to fall. I wanted to throw the window open to join in the fun. I longed for our old life together.

At the legation, we had food but no mattresses or blankets. I slept in a canvas chair, wrapped in my overcoat, sharing a tiny room with a young woman named Magda. A few nights after my move to the legation, the vicar of St. Matthew's Cathedral, who also happened to have an apartment in the building where Jóska and I lived, came over. I looked at him, thinking he had put on an awful lot of weight.

"Your husband sent you a little something," the vicar smiled as he threw his winter coat open. I was delighted to discover that he had my favorite warm blanket wrapped around his waist.

Laci also came to see me to talk me into staying at the papal legation as long as possible. He said the German soldiers were getting more and more cruel and were making Jewish women lick the soles of their boots. I flinched at the memory of my experience, but said nothing.

Most people still could not believe that these things were happening to others all around them. In reality, cruelty was rapidly unleashed and reverting to normalcy seemed impossible.

As the fall of 1944 wore on, Allied forces advanced north through Italy, with the Germans yielding inch by inch, fighting fiercely.

Ever since the Normandy landings in June, most Hungarians believed that the war would end in victory for the Allies. Jóska and I expected that American troops would be marching into Budapest. Estimates of the time varied greatly, and we often lost hope of being able to survive until that day.

In the ensuing weeks, the Allied bombing of Budapest intensified. The legation walls shook as explosions rocked the neighborhood. I fretted that the girls would be frightened without me in the basement shelter across the street, though I knew that they, like me, depended on Jóska for their security. The legation personnel had been assigned to a shelter under St. Matthew's Cathedral a block away. Of course, those of us who were in hiding couldn't be seen going there, so we endured the raids as best we could. Often plaster would fall on us like rain, and our scalps itched a lot of the time as a result. Little or no water was available for drinking, let alone for hair washing, since the water pipes had been severed by the shelling.

The German troops grew more desperate. The enforcement of every new decree, including the one that had ordered me to report to the sports stadium, diminished after a while, and the Nazis would think up some new form of torment.

When I had been in hiding for six weeks, Jóska related one evening that nearly all the Jewish women we knew who were married to non-Jews had stayed away from the roll call. Those who reported to the stadium had been deported. Those who stayed away had hidden in various places but were returning to their homes as time passed.

"No new summons has been issued," he said, "nor any mention that so many people disobeyed the orders.

"Livia and Ági keep asking for you. I'm running out of excuses. We all miss you," he told me.

Much as I knew that he loved me, he had seldom said those words to me of late. I felt tears welling up in my eyes, but managed to keep my voice under control.

"Do you think I would be endangering you or the children if I came home?"

"I don't think it would make any difference one way or the other," Jóska replied. "There seems to be no order, no follow-up on any of the decrees anymore. Why don't you just come home?"

"I'll come before dawn while the soldiers are sleeping," I promised, referring to the encampment in the square.

Dozens of rumors circulated on my last night at the legation. Some said the German army was in chaos; others felt Hitler would hold out to the last man. The residents listened with equanimity. Though my stomach churned at the thought of crossing the square to go home, to a great extent I had become numb and hardened by this time.

That night, an old man was admitted to the legation. He had taken refuge several months earlier at the Portuguese embassy. That embassy had been closed, the diplomats recalled to Portugal, and those sheltering there told to leave. Now the man had nowhere to go. Some of the priests became quite concerned, whispering that this man was still a practicing Jew.

"What shall we do? Should he be asked to go to daily Mass

like the others? What shall we tell His Excellency?" one of them inquired.

Later, I overheard the wise nuncio say to the priest, "Would you just leave him alone, please? He is a tired old man. Let him rest." *Something Jesus might have said,* I ruminated. *What a comfort it must be to be a true believer. But then again, the pope kept silent in the face of evil. I wouldn't want to believe his teachings! The Jews, on the other hand, keep waiting for a messiah, who never comes. I think what I am is an agnostic,* I reflected, and remembered that Apu had once told me agnostics believe that any ultimate reality is unknown. He had looked up the word in the dictionary and discovered it right above the words "Agnus Dei" (the lamb of God)—Christ the Savior. He found some irony in that, as I recalled. I felt what really mattered was to do our best for the people with whom we came in contact. There were too many real problems in our lives to spend too much time worrying about the unknowable.

That night, between air raids, my young roommate Magda's fiancé came to see her. Palcsi, who was an army officer, sat by his bride to-be. She had been sleeping on the floor beside me. He related that most of the foreign legation personnel were fleeing as the Soviet army approached from the east. He looked upset, and when Magda asked what was the matter, he told her he needed to see a priest. She found Father Matthew and brought him to our room.

"Do you want Éva and me to wait outside, Palcsi?" Magda asked.

"No, you need to hear what I have to say. All Hungarian army officers have been ordered to take the loyalty oath to Szálasi," Palcsi blurted out. Szálasi, the leader of the Arrow Cross Party, knew that the Germans couldn't hold Budapest much longer and was trying to accomplish all the Nazi plans in the time still left to him.

"Look, my son," Father Matthew said, addressing the young officer, "just go ahead and take the oath. Don't forget, you are not giving your word to God—only to Szálasi."

Palcsi appeared relieved as he walked with Magda to the front door.

Thoughts of my predicament kept me from sleeping. I had been hiding at the legation for six weeks: I had disregarded the order to report to the stadium; German soldiers were encamped on our doorstep. Was I endangering my family if I went home? On the other hand, there had been no follow-up on the order to report to the stadium. Jóska had told me that the BBC news broadcasts confirmed our suspicion that the Germans were losing the war and that their organization was disintegrating. Innumerable rumors circulated through the city. Many Jews were still in the ghetto houses, and no one knew why they had not been shipped out. At the legation, there was talk of papal intervention, big money changing hands, astronomical bribes from Sweden, Hitler having a Hungarian girlfriend besides Éva Braun, and other stories. I decided to take the risk and go home as planned.

Before dawn, I stuffed my belongings back in my shopping bag and quietly slipped out into the street. I glanced at what had been my temporary home and had to stop myself from running back inside. I crossed the square unobserved by sentries who patrolled around the parked trucks and tents in which the German encampment slept. Shadowy figures, real or imagined, appeared around me. The security I had felt at the legation receded with every step I took toward home. I stumbled while climbing the stairs to our apartment and heard my steps echo in the darkness. The walk home took no more than a couple of minutes, though an eternity passed before I unlocked our front door and entered.

To my delight, the girls jumped up and down with joy when they saw me in the morning. It was good to do the simple things that day—bathe them and say goodnight—then sitting in the living room with Jóska listening to the BBC on the shortwave.

A few days later, Jóska decided to bring my mother and father out of the ghetto house and hide them. He showed no fear at the prospect. He simply waited until evening to walk the kilometer or so to where they were housed. I paced the floor while he was gone.

My mother later told me that Jóska ripped the Star of David from my parents' coats and instructed them to look confident while they walked out their front door with him. No one questioned them. Their friend, Alice Mercer, who had been appointed to head the local Red Cross, offered to take them in. We hardly worried about my father. Being blond and blue-eyed, no one would suspect him of being Jewish. My mother, on the other hand, had inherited her shadowy beauty from her Ashkenazi ancestors. She would need to stay out of sight.

My parents were overjoyed to get out, even though they could not leave the Mercer house. Alice saw to it that they had everything. Whenever reliable friends came to see her, she let my parents out of their attic hiding place to enjoy the visitors.

Jóska and I felt responsible for Apu and Mother since we had relocated them. There were rumored house-to-house searches. Almost every day the Nazis broadcast a new date for rounding up remaining Jews in the city. That day would come and pass, and we would sigh with relief once again.

We felt that my parents should have some kind of false identification in case the bombings intensified and they had to leave their hiding place.

When my father wanted me to go get him some papers, Jóska put his foot down. This was one of the rare occasions when he expressly forbade me to do something.

"You have two children to think of; I won't let you do it. He must do it himself."

Transylvanian refugees were pouring into Budapest ahead of the Russian army. My father went to the Transylvanian Refugee Organization and in no time was supplied with a perfect set of false papers for Mother and him.

As winter approached, air raids became almost continuous

during daylight hours and sometimes even at night. At first, warnings would sound, but as time went on and wave after wave of bombers delivered their load, most people moved into the shelters on a more or less permanent basis. Since there were fewer raids at night, we continued to sleep in the apartment, while spending increasing time during the day in the shelter. Located below our basement, separated from it by five feet of solid rock, the shelter had been excavated during the early days of the war.

Shortly before the war, someone's maid had inadvertently stumbled into an abandoned stairway and discovered a complex of labyrinths that connected numerous underground chambers. Ten thousand residents of our neighborhood, including us, were now using these chambers as air raid shelters. Even under all that protection, we could hear the percussion from the exploding bombs. When one landed close by, the earth shook and loosened dirt rained on us.

"Come, children," Jóska called out during one of the earliest air raids that we spent underground. A dozen youngsters gathered around him. "Let's see if you can drown out all that noise." Then he burst into the Hungarian version of "Old MacDonald" and was soon joined by the children who sang at the top of their lungs. It became routine for the children to flock to Jóska the minute they heard warning of an attack or sounds of explosions. Their voices eased their parents' anxiety as well as their own.

The caves extended under a ten-mile portion of the Buda District where we lived. Hot springs had created the caves half a million years ago. During the Turkish invasions in the fifteenth century, when most of the population of Budapest sought shelter underground, tunnels had been dug to connect the caves under the cellars of the houses in the area. These shelters now extended under entire neighborhoods.

At various times during the siege, the cave under our cellar housed all eight families who lived in the building. We divided the space so each family had about a six- by-twelve-meter area to sleep, eat, and store their belongings. Most people left their possessions in the basement above and used the shelter only for sleeping. As supplies dwindled, however, more and more people tried to keep their remaining food with them, and the shelter became extremely crowded. The walls were damp, toilet facilities nonexistent. The children found the morning bucket brigade up the basement stairs amusing. The adults tried hard to retain some dignity during the process, some of them draping themselves with towels as they did delicate balancing acts over the buckets.

Jóska and I tried to continue normal routines as much as possible, listening to the BBC at night in our apartment and wondering whether we would live to see the end of it all. We spent most of our time trying to hunt down provisions, standing in line at the few stores that were still open and tracking down rumors of shipments of fruits and vegetables.

The children accepted our deteriorating circumstances without complaint. Livia continued to follow Jóska around wherever he went, drawing strength from his strength, relying utterly on his decisions. He had stopped working at the museum while I was in hiding. Besides, it had become increasingly difficult to go back and forth across the river. We were afraid that the bridges might be blown up at any time, in which case—since even small fishing boats had been commandeered by the military—he would be trapped on the other side. Jóska did not return to work even after I came home from the papal legation.

Both girls apparently felt that we would take care of them no matter what happened. They seemed secure in spite of the turbulence around our lives.

In the shelter, frayed nerves caused people's tempers to flare over minor incidents, usually involving children. One night Ági and some others tied the shoelaces of a sleeping neighbor together, causing him to stumble and fall when he woke up and tried to stand. Another night the girls swiped a sleeping woman's laces and used them as wicks in candles they were making out of drippings, much to the dismay of the shoes' owner.

Cleanliness became an increasing problem since the water mains had broken and we had no running water. Most people in the shelter were battling head lice, which caused us to itch to distraction. We rubbed our scalps with benzine and cut our hair very short, however, so the dead lice could be harvested by hand. Livia would put her head in Jóska's lap and let him pick off the offending creatures. Ági made it a point never to scratch her head when she thought we might be watching. She hoped thereby to avoid the only available treatment.

I had cooked a big batch of dried beans and invited our friends, Bebe and Laci, to come to our apartment for dinner. They arrived between air raids and remarked how amazingly casual we all were when discussing life-and-death issues.

"If they come for Éva, I think the time has come to use your gun," Laci told Jóska.

On that note, they left. I remember asking Jóska what he would do with the bodies.

"We have the key to the Denks' apartment, don't we?" he said. Our next-door neighbors had fled to Germany.

We left it at that. More weeks passed. No one bothered me. The building manager, whom we had suspected of being a Nazi sympathizer, seemed reliable after all.

One dreary November day, I met Pista, Jóska's youngest brother, walking across the square in front of our house. He, like most high-ranking Hungarian officers, had greatly admired Hitler's sensational organizational ability, but now was completely disillusioned.

"I am just back from Gondollo," he said, referring to the

summer home of the reigning Hungarian regent. "The retreating Germans have destroyed the palace for no reason."

Pista too had become aware that the German organization had broken down and that the end was fast approaching. We briefly discussed the idea that he could get false papers and disguise his identity before the Allies came.

"You can stay in the Denks' apartment and no one will be the wiser, Pista. They'll take you for a civilian," I told him.

Little did unwitting General Denk, safe in Germany, imagine the multiple uses envisioned for his lovely apartment.

Pista shook his head. "I can't abandon my men. It's impossible." With a wistful look, he kissed me on the cheek and left.

András

One day in November 1944, we heard knocking on our front door between air raids. We had taken the girls upstairs to find relief from the dank shelter. Since I'd had a great deal of difficulty sleeping for several weeks and didn't want to disturb Jóska with my tossing and turning, I had taken to sleeping in our spare bedroom. That day, I had set our lunch on a table there. It was the smallest room in the apartment, with only one window, and our body heat made it more comfortable than the living room or dining room. We had ceased trying to heat more than minimally due to a shortage of fuel. The wood or coal had to be lugged up four flights of stairs from the cellar, since the elevators had stopped working.

András and Margit were at the door. I had a feeling of foreboding when I saw them for the first time in many months. András had been organizing the Hungarian resistance, trying to promote the American advance, stave off the Russians, and sabotage the Germans.

We exchanged hugs after I let them in.

"It's great to see you, Éva. We have been on the move for weeks," András said. "Can you put us up for a few days?"

"Of course," I answered, handing him the keys to the Denks' apartment. "You'll be right next door and will have some privacy. The tenants went back to Germany months ago." I led them across the hall to the Denks' front door.

"Do you know anyone among the military who is completely reliable?" András asked.

I gave him the names of a couple of friends without inquiring why he wanted to know. The less one knew in those days, the less one could reveal in case of arrest and torture. András and Margit entered the Denks' apartment, and I left them to get settled.

As various problems had arisen over the past year concerning

Jewish relatives and friends, Jóska and I had always done what we could to help, without necessarily consulting each other.

My cousin Peter, who had been swindled by the Japanese chauffeur, couldn't get out of the country. Yoshi had taken all of Peter's money, then departed with the Japanese delegation. Peter hid in someone's attic and sent word through his benefactor asking that Jóska and I try to get his mother out of the Tolna ghetto. Jóska replied that he would see what he could do.

I was outraged by Peter's request, having risked everything for him once already. But I could not bring myself to say anything to Jóska. When Jóska contacted people in the underground, he learned that Peter's mother was already dead.

Jóska had been out when András and Margit arrived, but I felt certain he would have wanted to help András. When he came home, I told him that András and Margit were staying a few days.

"Do you realize you have taken a terrible risk?" Jóska said. I was surprised by his strong reaction.

It occurred to me that Jóska might be involved in András' resistance activities and hadn't told me.

"Okay," I said. "You tell András that you don't want them here." Jóska reached over and patted my hand as if to say he didn't mean to upset me.

He wasn't about to turn away a good friend, so Margit and András remained next door.

The very next day, Margit became frightened during an air raid and wanted to go down to the shelter. András, at great risk to him, went down with her at her insistence.

András, though still quite distinguished looking, was balding. Margit had toned down her elegant way of dressing. Visitors often appeared in the caves under the cellar, so no one would have paid any attention to them except that András was lame, which made people notice him. There must have been someone who recognized him, since his face was quite well known. Rumors about underground activities were a topic of discussion in most households, and András' name frequently came up.

During air raids, we had become quite good at judging from the explosions how far away bombs were dropping and had decided not to go to the shelter. I played Rachmaninoff on the piano to drown out the blasts, so the children would not be scared.

"Something isn't right, I can feel it," András said to me the following evening. "I've been in all kinds of situations and was never nervous. Now I can't sleep. I can't put my finger on it, but something is wrong."

András asked me to meet with Laci, who was in the same cell of the resistance as he. They were trying to establish contact with the Russians to learn of their movements.

"Ask him whether the Soviet liaison agents came to the cell meeting yesterday," András instructed. I knew that if the answer was no, it meant the Russians were afraid the resistance had been compromised.

I arranged to meet Laci in an underground subway station. It was dark and deserted. The trains had ceased running months ago when the power stations had been hit. Rats scurried around in the tunnels, and Laci kept glancing over his shoulder at the slightest sound.

"Something is wrong," he said. "The Russians didn't come and didn't send word."

"András and Margit went down to the shelter for the air raid," I said. The veins on Laci's temples pulsated.

"Margit is jeopardizing András' life," he said. "He shouldn't be seen in public."

I went home and duly reported to András, minus Laci's last remark.

"I have teams of people working to disarm explosives that the

Germans have strapped under the bridges crossing the Danube," András told me. "The Nazis intend to detonate each bridge as the Russian troops advance over it. You know those bridges are hundreds of years old," he continued, his emotions about these national treasures clear from his voice.

"We have been in touch with the American forces and hope our people can help stave off the Russian advance until the American troops enter Hungary. It's becoming clearer every day that the Americans aren't coming. We must do everything we can to stop the suffering and to save whatever buildings and bridges of historic value still remain," András said.

"I'm afraid the Russians didn't come to the meeting because they received intelligence information of our group's betrayal to the Germans. I don't like the sound of that," he concluded.

By dinner the next night, Jóska had come down with the flu. I felt his burning forehead.

"Don't fuss over me, Éva," he said, brushing my hand away. "I'll be all right."

I knew he didn't want to upset us, but I couldn't help worrying about him. We were without adequate food or heat and had no proper medication. We shared what little we had with András and Margit. I remember making a mock meatloaf out of kidney beans, and feeling good when Andràs complimented me on it. Jóska ate two bites and left the rest.

I took his plate back to the kitchen and put some melted snow water on the stove to heat for the children's bath. Besides the broken water main, the hot water heater had burst and parts had become impossible to obtain.

"When this whole thing is over," András said after I rejoined our friends, "we'll all go down to the farm and play with the little girls."

"András," I said, "if you succeed, I doubt that you will have time for Cservölgy. You will be in the Royal Palace, trying to run the country."

András was completely devoid of any personal ambition. He had not given much thought to what part he would play should his plans succeed. I suspect he felt that time for him was running out.

During the third night that András and Margit spent in the Denks' apartment across the hall, I heard a knock on our door. I woke, groggy, having taken a barbiturate to help me sleep, yet in minutes became alert as I heard pounding on the door opposite as well. I grabbed my bathrobe and ran to the door. Jóska reached the door at the same time. I looked through the peephole. The backs of three Gestapo agents in black uniform were visible. Each held a flashlight in his hand.

"Look," I whispered, letting Jóska see for himself.

He covered my mouth with his hand, afraid that the men in the hallway would hear me.

"Wait," he whispered into my ear, "András let them in."

Minutes passed without any sound from the hallway. We were frozen in our places, just inside our front door, afraid even to look through the peephole.

Then we heard the footsteps of several people walking down the stairs that led to the street.

We were still rooted there when Margit knocked, hysterical and sobbing. "They took him away," was all she could say when Jóska cracked the door open to let her in.

"I'm sure he'll be all right, Margit. He's a survivor," I lied.

"András can take care of himself," Jóska added.

"You know full well," Margit cried, "that he will not be all right."

There was little we could say, since all three of us knew what would happen to him. I hoped his death would be quick but knew better.

"We may well be next," Jóska verbalized what each of us had been thinking. He put his hand on my shoulder in a gesture of reassurance.

Would I be able to stand being tortured? I shuddered at the thought.

Once again depression and an unimaginable loneliness enveloped me. In spite of Jóska's presence, I knew that if they came for us, we would each be on our own.

Jóska still had the flu and was feverish. After settling Margit on the living room couch, I led him through the dark apartment. "Get under the covers," I told him and tucked an extra quilt around him.

"We'll make it through," he said, reaching up to touch my face.

I returned to the living room, not wanting to leave Margit alone with her thoughts. I brought her one of my precious stash of sleeping pills and sat with her, holding her hand.

"I had an affair once, Éva," she said out of the blue. "Do you think he knew?" Her eyes were moist as she looked at me.

"I have no idea, Margit," I replied. "You clearly love each other, so what difference does it make?" I thought it a bit strange for her to worry about such a thing at a time like this. She sank into a fitful sleep as the pill took effect.

Rhythmic wheezing sounds came from the bedroom. Jóska too had dozed off. I stared into the darkness. Artillery fire punctuated the night.

My mind raced. *Should we be waking the girls, taking them to hide somewhere? Where? What would I do if they came for Jóska? Would András survive? I'd heard about the kinds of torture the Nazis used—electrodes attached to genitals, healthy teeth drilled without anesthetic, fingernails pulled out. What if he gave them our names?*

Suddenly, I heard the girls crying, calling me to help them. They were in the street in front of the papal legation. I tried to run toward them but couldn't. They were being trampled by Nazi boots and were sinking into excrement. Livia's hand reached out to me and I tried to grab it, but it slipped through mine.

I woke with a start, shivering and shaking, having just let go of Margit's hand. I shook my head, trying to rid myself of the nightmare.

I felt my way to the boarded-up window and through a crack

peered out into the darkness. Nothing moved. It was hard to believe there were living, breathing, fearful people all around us, under curfew and blackout, just like us. I groped along the walls to the kitchen, not wanting to waken Margit or Jóska.

Since I knew that sleep would elude me, I sat by the table and, with the aid of a candle, made out notes for the girls to take to Bebe and Laci's home in case we were arrested. *How would they get there with all the shelling? Dear God, what would become of them?* When my appeal to God registered in my brain in the midst of all that anxiety, I found myself smiling at something Apu had once quoted me: "There are no atheists in foxholes." I guess he was right. If there was a god, where was he? Jóska was the one I believed in.

I could not stand to be alone another minute, so I slipped into bed beside Jóska without waking him. I stayed awake the rest of the night, waiting for the knock on the door, but the night passed and no one came for us.

At dawn, I realized that I needed to do something to warn others in the resistance that András had been arrested. (Later Laci told us the Nazis had picked up three other leaders during the night.)

Neither Jóska nor I could risk being seen in the street since the house was probably under surveillance. As soon as the children woke up, we gave Livia, who was then ten years old, a paper bag and sent her to Bebe and Laci's apartment. We told her that if anyone confronted her, she should say she was taking a piece of butter to Bebe *néni*. I had placed a note in a hollowed-out cube of butter, telling Bebe and Laci that András had been picked up during the night. We hated to send a child on such an errand, but we had no choice.

The girls looked at Margit, who was still asleep on the couch, but asked no questions. I put off until later giving them an explanation.

While Livia was gone, there was a furtive knock on the front door and there stood Laci. Margit awoke at the sound.

"I've come to warn András," he said, stepping into our entryway. "He must leave at once. There's been a leak."

"They took András away at two this morning," I replied.

We stood and looked at each other. Then Laci took sheets and scraps of paper out of his pockets. "Do you have a fire going?"

"Yes." I pointed towards Jóska's room where I had made a fire in the wood-burning stove. "Oh my God, Laci. You know you shouldn't be writing things down. What if you had been arrested?"

"It couldn't be helped," he muttered. He burned all his notes and left at once. To my great relief, Livia returned, having delivered the cube of butter and the message to Bebe in Laci's absence. She wiggled free when I gave her too long a hug, and went to find her sister.

Livia and Ági fluctuated between acting very grown-up, understanding the gravity of our situation, and the next minute acting like typical children ten and eight years old. A few days after Livia delivered the butter to Bebe, I heard her tell Ági that she had licked the cube on her way there as though it were an ice cream cone, and how delicious it had tasted. I had been hoarding that cube since it was our last.

We knew nothing and heard nothing of András until early December, when a government news broadcast announced that he and three others had been hanged. No reason was given.

A few days later Margit was on our doorstep, her formerly auburn hair completely gray. She was hysterical, incoherent, talking about a finger. It took a while to calm her to a point where she could explain what she was talking about. She had been moving around, staying with friends and relatives since András' arrest.

"Two Nazi officers came and knocked on the door at my sister's apartment," she said, ignoring our invitation to come in. "I was there alone, terrified. So like the knock the night they took András."

She broke down again and then a few minutes later resumed.

"I was afraid they'd break the door down, so I opened it. The Nazis clicked their heels and one of them handed over a box. 'These are your husband's remains,' he told me.

"I took the box from him, relieved that at least I would have his ashes. The officers kept standing there, and though they said nothing, I felt they wanted me to open the box."

She paused and bit the knuckles on her tightly clenched fist so hard that a trickle of blood ran down her hand. I started toward her, but Jóska gently put his hand on my arm and said, "Let her finish, Éva."

"I opened the box, expecting an urn," Margit continued, "but instead there was András' blood-stained finger with his wedding ring still on it. I could not, would not, let those animals see me break down. So I just kept quiet. They clicked their heels and said, 'Heil Hitler,' then turned and left me."

I took Margit by the hand and led her inside our apartment. Jóska shut the door, then turned around and enveloped her in his arms. I could see the vein on his temple pulsating and knew the anger and sorrow he must be feeling at the loss of his friend. My own heart was pounding, and I was sick with revulsion at the thought of what the Nazis had done and what Margit had endured.

There must be a special hell reserved for people who could do such things. I glanced at Jóska and saw tears streaming down his ashen face.

Margit left shortly to return to her sister Bianka's house before the nightly curfew. I met Bianka a few days later between air raids, while out foraging for food.

"I found Margit lying in a pool of blood," she told me. "She slit her wrists." I felt only the icy wind, nothing more.

Christmas 1944

Then came a bleak Christmas Eve, 1944. Jóska claimed he felt better, but he looked thin and worn. My mother and father risked leaving their hiding place at Alice Mercer's house to join us. Bebe and Laci came, and we pretended to be cheerful for the sake of the children.

Jóska had brought a live tree with us from the farm when we came to the city in September and had nursed it along in a bucket of dirt. We decorated our tree with glass balls, angel hair, and hand-painted glass birds. I clipped on traditional candles. "We shouldn't be using those," Jóska said. "We will need them to see by before the war is over."

"I know," I told him, "but the children would be so disappointed." Jóska shook his head but said nothing further and the candles stayed on the branches.

I risked leaving the apartment to try to find a Christmas treat for Livia and Ági, but failed in my attempt. As I returned home that afternoon, I met a young German soldier from the encampment outside the house. I had noticed him eyeing the girls on previous occasions when they played on the sidewalk between air raids. I suspected he was not much older than Livia and would have liked to join in the children's games.

"My name is Johann," he said, passing me a paper bag as I headed into the building. "The contents are for the children, *Gnädige Frau*."

I looked inside and discovered two little teddy bears, wearing lederhosen.

"Where on earth did you get these?"

"They came to our barracks in a box marked 'wool socks'!" Johann laughed.

"What an auspicious mistake. The girls will love these. Thank you so much, Johann," I said, touched by his gesture. "We had nothing to give them."

"My pleasure, *Gnädige Frau*," he replied. "Happy Christmas."

I glanced over his shoulder at the pockmarked buildings and our street dotted with shell craters. There seemed to be an unofficial ceasefire for the holiday. A blessed quiet had descended.

"Perhaps you'll be home next Christmas," I said to Johann, and his young face lit up. We parted without further comment, and I went upstairs.

I took out some Christmas paper that had been tucked away with the ornaments, wrapped up the bears, and put them under the tree.

"How ironic that the Germans are providing our children's presents," Jóska mused when I told him the source of the gifts.

"It's a crazy world, isn't it?"

"Guess who is fraternizing with them?" Jóska asked.

"I have no idea."

"I took the children outside to get some fresh air a while ago since there seemed to be a let-up in the shelling. Ági hung around the soldiers outside the house. I saw her swipe a couple of chocolate bars from the dashboard of one of their broken-down jeeps. To tell you the truth, I think Johann or one of the others left them there on purpose for the children to find."

"Did you say anything to her?" I asked.

"No. I didn't have the heart to make her give them back."

Ági tended to be more aware of what was going on than Livia. She spent a lot of time listening to adults and seemed to take in what we discussed. From the time she was very small, I thought of her as a midget adult rather than as a child. While Livia followed Jóska without question, Ági worked on supplying us with various necessities by charming the soldiers out of some of their rations. She produced a bag of popcorn for dessert that night. It smelled and tasted wonderful.

When our guests left the apartment, I tugged aside one of the boards covering the windows to look at the sky. As I stood there admiring the crystal-clear sky, I heard the big guns up close for the first time. The Russians must be very near. All that we hoped for was not to be. *The Americans aren't going to get here in time,* I thought. The Russian army closed its juggernaut that night, encircling Budapest.

None of us were then aware that at the Yalta Conference in November, Churchill, Roosevelt, and Stalin had agreed that Hungary would be occupied by the Russian forces. The American advance would halt at the Elbe River in Germany.

There were no more air raid alarms; air raids had become continuous. Even the Germans set up makeshift beds for their troops in the cellars of the buildings in our neighborhood. Since November, the buildings' occupants, including ours, lived almost full time in the underground caves below the cellars. These caves, unused since the Turkish occupation centuries earlier, were thought to be bombproof. We tried to set up sleeping cots in the small space allotted to us in the cave under our building. It was always damp there, and sometimes water stood an inch deep, seeping from the walls.

During the first days of intensive raids in January 1945, bombs fell on the city's water main as well as the gas works. Now we had no water or gas in the apartment. A few days later, the city's power plant was hit, and the lights went out all over Budapest. We kept flipping on the switches out of habit, only to realize over and over that there were no lights. Our coal and wood supply had also run out. Jóska and I burned pieces of furniture in our wood-burning stoves to keep warm, and we melted snow for drinking. The cold winter was a mixed blessing. It supplied us with drinking water, but also made the temperature bone chilling.

We put candles on outcroppings and ledges along the shelter walls. The smell of wax mingled with that of mildew and unwashed bodies. We still tried to sleep upstairs in our apartment whenever there seemed to be a pause in the shelling. Then one night, when there was continuous bombing, we remained in the shelter until dawn.

Livia and Ági spent a lot of time gathering candle drippings. They held the wax in their hands until it softened and then shaped it into new candles, using pieces of string for wicks. When string ran out, they swiped and used shoelaces. Day by day, we accepted behavior that would never have been tolerated in times gone by.

The filth and smell in our apartment house and in the shelter were repulsive. People used an abandoned first-floor apartment as a latrine. During air raids, when we dashed past the apartment door on our way to the shelter, the girls would giggle if they heard people defecating. At least the steam heat wasn't functioning, and the temperature remained cold, so the situation was bearable. The Germans detailed some of their prisoners to shovel snow through the windows to try to cover the excrement. We had buckets in the apartment and in the shelter, since I couldn't bring myself to use that apartment, nor would I take the children there.

Most of us had head lice and itched to distraction. We had no water for bathing and precious little for drinking. Jóska hid a couple of jugs.

"I will shoot anyone who touches our water supply," he said. He tended not to be melodramatic, so I had no doubt that he meant what he said. He kept a hunting rifle locked up in the apartment. Only minor thefts had been reported up until then, but conditions were deteriorating.

On the whole, people were surprisingly calm. No hysteria, very little complaining about conditions—everybody just waited.

One morning Lali, the janitor's son, came to the shelter and excitedly told us that the butcher down the street had some horsemeat. When the shelling let up a bit, I went to stand in line outside the shop in the bitter cold. I clutched my coat tightly around me, but my boots leaked, and my feet froze as we shuffled forward at a snail's pace. Just as I reached the entrance of the shop, Mr. Biro, the butcher, appeared, blocking the door with his bulky frame.

"That's it, folks. There's no more. I'm sorry," he said and quickly shut the door before any of us could protest. I had hoped to have some fresh meat to give to the children. I hurried home empty-handed, walking close to the houses since the shelling had resumed.

As I entered the lobby of our building, a yellow notice on the wall caught my eye:

"The ground-floor apartments must be vacated by January 15, 1945, by order of the Commandant."

No explanation was given, just the notice. I wondered what the Germans were up to.

They commandeered space all over the city for their troops. Though we felt sorry for the ground-floor tenants, we were not personally concerned, since we lived on the fourth floor.

On January 15, much to the delight of the children, a dozen horses from a German Cavalry Division took up residence in one of the ground-floor units, next to the one being used as a latrine. Very young German grooms, no more than fifteen or sixteen years of age, took care of the animals. They too were caught up in the war, just like our girls. They made friends with Livia and Ági and allowed them to help feed the horses. The food consisted of a substance resembling sawdust. The animals looked emaciated and sick. Whenever we passed their stable, we could hear the horses stomping on the hardwood floors, moving about restlessly.

A few days later, the children and I went to pick up our ration of sugar at a distribution station about a block away. The girls wanted to carry their own little bags. As we returned home, Hans, one of the grooms, came toward us. Livia and Ági greeted him with enthusiasm.

"Are the horses doing all right?" Livia asked him in halting German.

"Fine, little miss," Hans replied.

I headed for the stairs, followed by Livia. As I turned the corner at the first landing, I glanced down behind me and saw that Ági was passing her bag of sugar to the groom.

"Give it to them," she said.

Much as we needed the sugar, I couldn't bring myself to reprimand her, so I said nothing. Moments later Ági caught up to me, taking the stairs two at a time with an innocent look on her face.

One night in January, Father Matthew, the young priest from the legation, approached me in our shelter.

"Excuse me," he whispered, all the while looking over my shoulder. "I have friends in the Arrow Cross Party, and they tell me that at dawn tomorrow, those considered to be half-breeds will all be picked up. I was wondering whether you and your children have false documents? If not, I might be able to..."

"Thank you, Father, we are very well equipped," I said, reassuring him, although his words sent a chill through me. He nodded and went up the stairs into the night. It was good to know that he was concerned about us.

Once again I felt real terror. *What if my false papers didn't pass muster?* I tossed and turned that night on the narrow cot in the shelter, dreading the possibility.

Later Bebe, in similar circumstances as our children, with a Jewish father and a gentile mother, told me that the janitor at their building came to their apartment the same night to warn her.

The next day crept by, and nothing happened. Once again, the ever-present threat receded into the background, pushed aside by daily survival concerns.

The Germans were handing out leaflets describing the terrible things the Russians were doing as their armies advanced into Hungary. The leaflets told about raping and looting. We feared what the future would hold, even if the Russians arrived before the Nazis caught up with me.

Burning Horses

Cannons had been firing for days on end, from the Pest side of the Danube, across to Buda where we lived. The rumble of cannon fire could be heard even in the shelter. As bombs cascaded on the neighborhood, the bedrock above us reverberated, dumping dirt and pebbles of stone on us. We wondered if the cave would collapse should the building above us sustain a direct hit.

On New Year's Eve, the Germans parked trucks loaded with barrels of gasoline up against our apartment building. Jóska and some of the other tenants urged them to no avail to move the trucks to the center of the square. We worried that the gasoline would be ignited and the fire trap us in the shelter, if one of the trucks were hit.

It only took two days for our worst fears to be realized. We had spent the night in the caves and, in the early morning of January 2, 1945, heard an enormous explosion. The ground shook. Then we felt a series of blasts as the drums ignited, one by one. The barrels, we were told later, had flown into the air and then burst apart, spewing flames in all directions.

One of the neighbors cried out in alarm. I hugged the children to me. We surmised that either an incendiary bomb or a cannon blast had hit its mark and set off the chain reaction. In seconds, we heard crackling sounds that provided a muted background to the continuing explosions; the building above us had caught fire.

The smell of gasoline filled the air. Some people in the shelter headed for the ladder, hoping to save belongings from their apartments before the fire spread. A few made it, returning carrying suitcases; others perished in the fire.

Jóska and I had a change of clothing for ourselves and the children in two suitcases stacked under our cots. We made no attempt to go up to our apartment.

Those returning to the shelter reported that the front and back doors leading out of the building were blocked by fire.

"Bring the girls. I'll get our bags," Jóska instructed. "Our only hope is to go through the passage to the shelter next door."

At that moment, István Pataki, a writer who lived in the apartment below ours, came down the ladder, dragging a huge suitcase. It burst open, and hundreds of pages of manuscript fluttered out. His wife followed him down, her face and hands red and blistered from the heat of the fire. Behind them came a lady who lived in apartment 3D. She looked bewildered and carried only a red lampshade.

Smoke poured through the opening where the ladder was, and people started coughing. I took the children by the hand. We followed Jóska into the tunnel connecting our cave to the one beneath the house next door. Within moments, people were piling up behind us, pressing forward. The man following me was breathing on my neck. I felt trapped. The girls held tightly to my hands.

We reached the makeshift door that separated the two shelters and discovered that it was blocked on the other side. Jóska pounded on the door. It was cracked open by one of the occupants. He glared at us.

"We have too many people in here already," He gestured behind him. "You can't come in!" he shouted, trying to shove the door closed again.

Jóska tried to force it open, but some of the occupants on the other side were leaning against it. The girls coughed and rubbed their eyes.

The smell of smoke mingled with that of burning flesh. We could hear a muffled rumbling sound. *We'll be buried in here,* I thought.

"Oh my God," I said, as the stink intensified. "The horses must be trapped upstairs!"

The image of burning horses overwhelmed me, and then I

visualized our burning, trapped in that tunnel, and, in spite of the crush of people shoving us forward, I shivered. I tightened my hold on the children's hands and shielded them from the crush of bodies behind us. I tried to appear calm for their sake.

Jóska pleaded with the people through the barricaded door, and at last they agreed to let us pass. We had to promise that none of us would stay in their shelter; we just wanted to go through to the street above. They opened the door, and we stumbled forward, eyes itching, coughing in the smoky air. The cellar next door was even more crowded than ours had been. People sat in chairs lined against the walls. They had no mats or cots, so I could understand their reluctance to admit us. We scrambled up their ladder and out into the street.

When we reached the square in front of our apartment house, the smoke from the fire blotted out the sun. In spite of it being a cold winter day, with snow piled along the gutters, the heat from the flames felt like a furnace blast in our faces. We joined a group of people milling around in the middle of the square. Some of them were injured, and others wandered around looking dazed. The front door of our building was blocked by burning debris. The second floor had collapsed into the first floor. Looking up, I saw flames reaching out with blue and orange claws from our bedroom windows. They leaped skyward in a macabre dance.

I could hear the thumping of hooves against the floor and horses neighing in desperation. Then a sound—the likes of which I had never heard before or since—an eerie scream came from one of the dying horses.

The Germans were using axes on the brick wall to try to break through to release the animals. One wall collapsed, and what must have been the only surviving horse staggered out, mane aflame.

One of the soldiers drew his pistol, aimed, and fired. The horse staggered into a snow bank a few feet in front of us, collapsed and lay still, his head enveloped in flames. The snow sizzled, melting beneath his head, and a rivulet of blood, mingled with the snow, ran toward Ági's feet. The smell of burning hair and flesh filled the air.

Guilt and horror enveloped me. We should have urged the Germans to let the horses loose, rather than stable them in an apartment. Maybe at least a few of them would have survived. Ági stood transfixed, staring at the burning horse. "Come," I said to her, "let's get away from here."

She seemed unable to move. Jóska picked up Livia and the larger of two suitcases we lugged from the shelter, and motioned for me to take Ági. I picked her up, grabbed the other suitcase, and staggered across the street. We stood on the sidewalk, Jóska and I, each holding one of the girls by the hand, gazing back at the flaming inferno that had engulfed our home.

"All our food is gone," Jóska said. "I took what was left up to the apartment yesterday, since people were looting in the cellar."

"What can we do?"

"Perhaps Alice would put us up," Jóska said, referring to our friend, the lady who was giving shelter to my parents.

Livia stood gazing up at the flames leaping from our apartment. I too was mesmerized by the fire. For a moment, I envisioned how the girls had looked standing behind the safety bars of their bedroom window, waving to us on so many occasions when Jóska and I were either leaving or returning home. Now the bars were changing shape, curving, melting, and glowing because of the fire. The flames enveloped my vision of the girls, and I shuddered.

Father Matthew, who had offered to help with my papers a few days before, came out of the legation across the street. He carried a bowie knife and a yellow bowl. I realized that he was heading for the horse that had dropped at our feet a few minutes before: he was about to butcher it.

"We must get these girls away from this," I said.

"Perhaps the legation," Jóska answered, observing the priest. "Let's try."

The Church once again gave shelter to this agnostic Jew, this time with family in tow. When we knocked, a nun let us in. She unfolded some deck chairs, placing them in the common room, and told us we could stay. Half a dozen nuns ministered to the people in residence. Later, they prepared soup for us, using the horsemeat brought back by Father Matthew. *We will owe our soul to the Catholic Church before this war is over,* I thought.

We spent several nights at the legation, sleeping in the deck chairs or on the floor, not even trying to move into the overcrowded shelter under the cathedral. Shelling seemed continuous outside. All that was left of our belongings was in the two suitcases.

The nuns tended to various refugees from the bombed-out houses in the neighborhood who had moved in with the Jews already living at the legation. The sisters ordered us about, telling us what to do and asking the children to get out of their way. They were not unkind, but their actions impressed upon us that we had no home.

The girls had been quite happy as long as we were in our own house, even in the shelter. There they had friends from neighboring apartments and were given scraps of food by the soldiers encamped outside.

Strangely, all the bombing had not seemed to frighten them. I can still remember Ági shaking the bits of plaster out of her hair when the building shook and the ceiling crumpled for the umpteenth time. She made no comment about what was happening, just continued talking to me. At the legation, however, strangers surrounded them, and both children became very quiet and, for the first time, seemed scared.

A few days after our arrival at the legation, there was a lull in the fighting, and Jóska and I went out into a beautiful, cold winter day for a breath of fresh air. We stopped to talk to Lali, the janitor's seventeen-year-old son from our building, who had joined us on the sidewalk. Firing began again, and the three of us ran for the legation. Just as we reached the massive doors, a shell hit the brass plate on the door and fragmented. I felt a searing pain as shrapnel hit me in the head. Lali fell to the ground, wounded in the leg. Jóska grabbed me, but I knew right away that I was not seriously injured as the pain was already receding.

"I'm all right. Help Lali. He can't walk," I told Jóska. Blood trickled down my forehead.

As I pushed the door open and staggered inside, I looked back to see Jóska carrying the boy toward the emergency underground hospital which had been set up some months ago in the basement of St. Matthew's Cathedral up the street. I pressed a towel against my head to stop the bleeding.

Sister Josefina, a nursing nun working at the legation, saw my plight. "Let me help you, dear," she said. "Come with me." She guided me by my elbow to a small dispensary she had set up in a closet. "I need to shave some hair off your head, so I can clean the wound."

Sister Josefina lit a candle to provide some meager light, trying to get a look at the nasty gash. She set the candle on a shelf before she went to get some hot water from the kitchen. I sat there, staring into the flame: for a moment, the flicker dissolved and in it I saw myself sitting at the piano on my sixteenth birthday, hair shining, gypsy violins playing. How very long ago that had been.

Sister's voice brought me back to the present.

"It looks like just a small fragment. I won't try to remove it. Leave it alone, Éva, and on no account go near the emergency hospital."

It was a military hospital. Civilians who came there were given short shrift by the German doctors. It had never occurred to me to go there. So much had happened to me by this time that a bit of shrapnel in my skull was like a sneeze in normal times.

"They kept Lali at the hospital," Jóska told us when he returned safely from his errand of mercy. He hugged me, relieved to find out that I was all right.

The German troops, in disarray, had retreated to Buda where they were trapped along with us, surrounded by the advancing Russian armies. Filling the vacuum left by the Germans, the Pest side of the city was completely occupied by the Russians, giving them a straight shot at Buda across the Danube.

At the papal legation, conditions deteriorated. We continued to be under heavy bombardment and artillery attack. The building rained plaster on us as it shook. Getting a direct hit was only a matter of time.

The water supply in the Buda neighborhoods had almost completely run out. Jóska and I took turns walking through the labyrinths between the underground caves, hoping to find an undiscovered well. We kept meeting various people from neighboring houses, however, who were on the same unsuccessful errand. We discussed leaving our neighborhood to try to find shelter and water elsewhere.

Lali crawled back from the hospital on the same afternoon that he had been injured, dragging his broken leg behind him, and reported that conditions there were unbearable.

The legation's food supply had dwindled down to nothing but dried beans. We hadn't eaten any meat, except for the horse, or fresh food of any kind in weeks. Lali reported that he had seen another dead horse right in front of our burned house, across the square, perhaps abandoned by cavalry passing through the square, in search of an escape route. Somebody else said he had seen that particular horse being shot by a soldier. This was important information, because we tried to avoid eating horses that had died of questionable causes.

Armed with a crate one of the nuns provided, along with a sharp knife, I went out to get to the horse before other people had a chance to butcher it.

Snow was falling and the gunfire had ceased for the moment. I ran across the square, safely reaching the sidewalk. As I took a few more steps, I stumbled over the horse, partly covered by snow. I looked up at the burned-out windows of the children's former nursery. The blackness of the walls marked the termination of our former lives.

But where should I start carving on the horse? The firing began again. A couple of German soldiers came by, hurrying along the wall of our former home. I wasn't about to go back to the legation without some of the meat, shelling or no shelling.

"What's the most edible part of a horse?" I called to the soldiers.

They shrugged, but pointed to the hindquarters. The horse was still warm, and it gave me a creepy feeling to cut into it. These warriors must have been city boys, because they had given me the wrong advice. Here I was, kneeling in the snow, next to this dead horse, in the midst of shelling, trying to cut through tough sinew to find some edible meat. I must have severed an artery because warm blood spurted in my face, covering my glasses. I wiped them on the sleeve of my coat as best I could and kept hacking away.

In the end, I chopped a good ten or twelve kilos of fresh meat from the horse's haunches before anyone else appeared on the scene.

I headed back to the legation. In the doorway, I encountered one of the resident Monsignors, armed with a bowl and a knife. He looked a bit startled at my appearance, but said nothing. Bloody sights were common in those days.

"Interesting work in the service of the Lord," I said to him. He nodded, but made no reply. He headed off in the direction of the carcass.

The sisters cooked a stew by boiling the meat I'd brought and throwing in some of the dried beans. The concoction tasted wonderful.

The next morning, I decided to make my way to Jóska's brother Aurél's. Aurél and his family were living at the Technological University building where he worked and where there was a decent shelter. I was determined to walk the three-kilometer distance.

Jóska and I had discussed which of us should stay with the children. I convinced him that he would be better able to support the girls if something happened to me than the other way around. I took a hunk of cooked horse meat from the kitchen and set out for Aurél's. I managed to walk around the corner from the legation when artillery fire reached such a pitch that I felt I would never reach the university. I decided it would be smarter to stay with Jóska and the children and ran back inside.

The following day, without telling us, my parents set out from Alice's house and took the long walk to the Technological University. They brought us word that Aurél had food and was expecting us.

Jóska and I loaded the suitcases and the girls onto a toboggan that Jóska had stolen during the night, and we set out.

"Even the Church sanctions stealing, when it's to save your life," he said, with his old mischievous grin. It had been a long time since I'd seen him smile like that. Jóska had aged visibly over the winter and was coughing a lot. I was happy to see that he could still smile.

Jóska pulled the sled. On the way we met some Hungarian soldiers. They warned us that our route was within range of the Russian guns, and that the area appeared to be targeted. As we plodded on through the deserted streets, I kept having the feeling that someone was following us. I glanced back repeatedly but saw no one. Bullets whistled past our ears.

"Snipers," Jóska speculated.

"Should we turn back?" I asked him.

"We can't," he said. "We've got to have food.

"We'll be all right. Hunker down," my husband told the girls, trying to reassure them. He wanted them to present as small a target as possible. We kept on trudging through the snow, frightened and very cold. I again looked behind us and thought I saw someone duck into a doorway. I told Jóska, so we waited a few minutes but no one appeared, so we moved on.

We reached the Technological University without further trouble and found Aurél and his family in the shelter. We knew that the Russians would mount an all-out attack in a matter of days, possibly hours.

Aurél resembled their mother, whom I loved dearly, but who always saw things in a rosy light—in the way she wanted them to be. Aurél had told my parents that there was plenty of everything. In reality, he hid the little food they had, keeping it for his children.

Aurél did offer to let us stay with them in their shelter. Two other faculty families were already living there, together with Aurél, his wife Maria, and his two children. The four of us brought the number to nineteen people. We tried to be as inconspicuous as possible as we brought in our possessions from the toboggan.

When my parents had moved to the ghetto house from their Buda home, they had left some food (flour, lard, sugar, and other staples) for safekeeping at their neighbor's house. I decided to risk the walk to Somlolyi út, the street where they used to live, and see whether there was anything left. I went at dusk, hoping to present less of a target and arrived without incident.

After I knocked persistently on the neighbors' door, it was finally cracked open and, much to my surprise, Borcsa néni peered out at me.

When she saw me, she opened the door and threw her arms around me. Though she looked old and frail, it thrilled me to see her. I brought her up to date on Mother, Apu, Jóska, and the children. She in turn told me she had returned to her family shortly after my parents had to give up their home.

"My sister was in service in this house, with the Dobos family," she explained to me between sobs. "She's dead now." Borcsa *néni* blew her nose to compose herself. "Didn't you know they were all killed?"

"I'm so sorry, Borcsa *néni*," I mumbled.

"Everyone died—except the baby," she continued. "Their son-in-law had decided to move all seven of them, the family and my sister, to his military barracks. He thought they'd be better protected there. I came here to keep an eye on the house. A bomb shattered the whole building where they were staying, killing them all, except for Katinka."

Tears ran down Borcsa *néni*'s cheeks as she spoke. A small, golden-haired toddler appeared from behind a door and smiled at me. How I wished that I could help this child and this old woman, who linked me to my past.

My eyes became moist at the sight of Katinka, the tiny survivor. Not trusting my voice, I waved to her.

"I wish..." I started to say, but Borcsa *néni* hugged me again and said, "I'll make you a whipped cream cake when this is over, child." I realized that I would always be a little girl to her. I clung to her for a moment and then left.

I retraced my steps down the hill, thinking of good times before the war. It wasn't until I approached the Technological University that I realized I had not asked about the food left by my parents, and Borcsa *néni* hadn't asked why I had come.

The firing started again and became so intense that I stood for some time close to the wall of a house and waited. Then I remembered that there was a convent close by, and I ran and knocked on the door.

A young sister answered, quite agitated. "Our kitchen's on fire!" she exclaimed.

Nuns scurried about, carrying buckets of water, heading toward the back of the building. The fire had nothing whatsoever to do with the war. Some spilled grease had ignited. I asked the sister for some bread, and she hurried off and found me a loaf. *Wonder of wonders,* I thought—*a whole loaf of bread.* I didn't return empty-handed after all. I ran back to the university and hid the loaf from Aurél's children.

How low we had sunk—stealing a toboggan and now hiding bread from each other. I pondered what the nuns who had given me the bread would think, if they knew. *I'm inflicted with a double dose of guilt, being in effect a Jewish Catholic,* I mused. But then I thought, *even if I believed in either religion, which I did not, neither condemned doing what is necessary to save one's life.*

Rumor mills operated full time, as block by block the city fell to the Red Army. Some Russian soldiers had been spotted crossing the Danube by boat. Many of their comrades had been killed when the bridges were blown up as they attempted to cross to the Buda side of the river.

"I'm glad András didn't live to see this day," Jóska told me.

"He loved those bridges and wanted so much to save them," I replied.

The remaining German troops were in a panic. Many of the young ones stole civilian clothes, trying to pass for Hungarians. Suicides were commonplace.

Rumors of looting and raping preceded the Soviet troops. With the coming of winter, the lice epidemic had subsided, so we had allowed the girls to let their hair grow. Once the Russian conquest became imminent, we cut off Livia and Ági's hair again and dressed them in pants, hoping they would pass for boys and be left alone.

The Russian Nightmare

On February 14, 1945, whenever someone attempted to open the door to go upstairs from the shelter, we could hear rifle fire from the street.

"I'm going to try to have a look at what's going on," Jóska said, heading for the cellar door that opened onto some outside stairs and led to the street. As he cracked the door open, we heard a bullet ricochet off the metal guardrail. Jóska ducked back inside.

"A German soldier is stripping off his uniform in the stairwell, and I saw a Russian dodging into a doorway across the street," he said. "They must be fighting house to house at this point."

"How long before it's all over, do you suppose?" I asked him.

"I suspect they can't last more than a couple of hours," Jóska replied, referring to the Germans.

We exchanged glances, wondering what the Russian occupation would be like, but not wanting to discuss it in front of the children. There had been rumors of grenades being thrown into cellars.

An eerie silence descended within the hour after Jóska's attempt to go upstairs. At nightfall, we heard a polite knock on the cellar door. I took the children by the hand when I felt a tension pervade the shelter's occupants. Jóska's brother, Aurél, a tall, lanky man with an unblinking gaze, stepped forward and slowly opened the door. A handsome Russian officer walked into the cellar. What then ensued was nothing like what we had imagined.

"*Jó estét*" (good evening), the officer said, greeting us all in fluent Hungarian. He shook hands with the male occupants and asked where his men could be quartered.

"The building upstairs is full of dead horses, unloaded there by the retreating Germans," Jóska replied. "As you know, it's been bitterly cold, so the horses have not yet decomposed. However, the place is not fit for human habitation."

The Russian said he'd look elsewhere for housing, and departed.

"What a relief," Aurél said, echoing my thoughts.

"Don't get too excited," Jóska warned. "What comes next may be very different."

"Can we go outside?" the girls asked in unison.

"No," Jóska told them. "We must be patient."

About half an hour later, a group of Russian soldiers came in. They all wore dark mustard-colored uniforms, showing no designation of any rank. They pointed to our watches and gestured at any jewelry anyone was wearing. Though we had no language in common, we understood they wanted these items. The news that the invading troops were partial to watches had preceded them, so we were not surprised.

Those in the shelter, who had not hidden their valuables, handed them over. My watch had been lost in the fire, but Jóska had his and had strapped it around his ankle several days before in anticipation of the arrival of the Russian troops. A couple of the young Russians made me very uneasy when they eyed the girls and looked me up and down. I had a hunch Livia and Ági's delicate features belied their boyish haircuts and clothing. Much to our relief, however, the soldiers made no move toward us. After a few minutes, the Russians sauntered out of the shelter.

Jóska and Aurél went to try to find the Hungarian-speaking officer and spotted him at the other end of the huge complex that comprised the Technical University. He had commandeered some space there.

"Tell the people to hide their jewelry," he said in response to Jóska and Aurél's complaints of looting by his soldiers. The brothers came back to the shelter, not particularly reassured by their discussion with the Russian.

What happened next demonstrates the mixed emotions and

loyalties engendered by our wartime experiences. Germany was an official ally of Hungary. Our troops were fighting on their side. Many of the German soldiers had been kind to our children during the siege of Budapest. In spite of their brutality toward the Jews, the Germans were fellow Europeans, a known entity. We regarded the conquering Russian troops as barbaric hordes.

Johann, the young German soldier who had given the teddy bears to the girls for Christmas, came dashing down the shelter stairs. *He must have been the person who had followed us on our way to Aurél's,* I thought.

"I need someplace to hide," he begged, dread reflected in his eyes. Aurél stuck him between a mattress and the floor. At Jóska's hurried instructions some of the children, including Livia, sat on the mattress.

A big bear of a Soviet soldier followed Johann into the cellar by seconds. The Russian must have known that we had hidden the boy, because he headed straight for the bed, gestured for the children to get off. He stuck his bayonet through the mattress. We held our breath, hoping he'd miss Johann. The only noise came from the Russian's arm, where half a dozen watches were ticking. No sound from beneath the mattress, only a slight movement. The Russian grinned and thrust his bayonet again and again.

I cringed with each thrust, imagining the blade passing through flesh. Livia clutched Jóska's hand, and Ági hid behind me. I could feel a rivulet of perspiration run down between my shoulder blades. Not a word from the Russian, just a leer, as he turned and stomped back up the stairs, waving the blood-smeared bayonet as he went.

Aurél pulled aside the mattress. Johann's heart had been pierced, probably by the first thrust, since he had not uttered a sound. His eyes, wide open, were filled with terror. Blood oozed from his wounds, seeping from beneath his body onto the floor. Jóska stepped forward and gently closed the young soldier's eyes.

As he did so, he noticed something protruding from the boy's shirt pocket. He extracted a photograph of a girl, took a glance at it and, without a word, handed it to me. I saw that Johann's blood had stained the photo so that the girl appeared to be shedding tears of blood. Jóska reached for the picture and slipped it back into the boy's pocket.

Livia, standing beside me, burst into tears, and for once, even Jóska could not soothe her. She sobbed as he held her close for a long time. I myself felt even more desolate when I realized that Ági, who seemed to observe the bleeding boy with detachment, made a visible effort to control her emotions.

"He's better off dead anyway," she informed me.

I could not deny her statement, so I just put my arms around her and we stood, rocking back and forth, staring at the scene before us. Two of the men wrapped the body in a blanket and took it away.

At four o'clock in the morning, a group of soldiers with Mongolian features, wearing the same dark mustard-colored uniforms without insignia, came and at gunpoint took two young women from the shelter. Like men the world over, they seemed most interested in young, pretty girls. They glanced at my wedding ring and the children and left me alone. The girls were frightened, and they held onto my ski pants which I was wearing to keep warm. I had told Jóska earlier to please promise me not to try any heroics should anything happen to me. It would not help any of us if he were killed. There was no need to mention that we would both give our lives to save our children, if that became necessary.

As compared with the German occupiers, the Russians were uncivilized, taking what they pleased and whom they pleased.

The first full day of the Russian occupation dawned. For us, the war was over and, in spite of the terror of the last twenty-four hours, I felt a great sense of relief. The Nazi nightmare had come to an end, and I felt much more like a normal person again.

We would make a fresh start, I thought. *Maybe I could get a job. Perhaps it would even help that we had been in the Resistance.* Aurél and Jóska thought we should try to establish some sort of contact with the occupying troops. The Hungarian-speaking officer had left the university compound with his men. Aurél begged me to go and try to talk to the Russians in French. French being the language of diplomacy at that time, there was some hope that someone at headquarters would understand me.

"Find out, for God's sake, where the headquarters are, so we can talk to someone in charge," Aurél told me.

No one at headquarters spoke French. No one that I could find had any insignia I could identify. This new thing, the army of occupation, seemed to be headless.

On my way back from a fruitless search to find some authority figure on the university grounds, a Hungarian man came by, wearing an armband that said "Interpreter." I stopped him, but then I noticed he was crying.

"Oh God, my wife was raped eight times last night. They are animals, animals," said the interpreter and kept on walking, muttering to himself. I felt hollow inside.

In a day or two, we found a deserted apartment located across the street from the university. The front of the building lay in ruins, having sustained a direct hit. A stairwell in the middle of it stood exposed to the street. Though some of the steps were damaged, we could make our way up the stairway to the second floor. There, toward the back of the building, we found a two-room furnished apartment intact. The door had been blown off, probably by the bomb blast that had destroyed the front of the building, but other than the layer of plaster dust that covered everything, the rooms appeared untouched. Jóska and I hesitated only the briefest moment before collecting the girls from the shelter and moving our possessions into the apartment.

It must have belonged to a woman because the overall impression was of pink frill. We took turns using the single bed that stood against the wall in the bedroom. The girls delighted in snuggling into it. It had been a long time since any of us had slept in a bed.

Though there might have been living space on the two floors above, the condition of the stairs was so precarious that we dared not check. We seemed to be alone in the building. We delighted in having found a roof to put over our heads. We felt uneasy at what might happen, however, if any of the frequent Russians patrols, on their rounds through the neighborhood, spotted us.

We had no water, no heat, and a minimum of food. We rationed the bit of rice and beans Jóska had managed to trade for his watch, not knowing how long we needed to survive on what we had left. We wondered whether conditions were better on the Pest side of the river and decided to go there, if we could find a way. All the bridges on the Danube had been blown up by the retreating German army, in spite of the Resistance's best efforts to save them.

Jóska and I had both lost weight over the past winter and felt tired all the time. We needed to find food. While the snow lasted, we had access to water and could at least make a soup by boiling beans with the rice. In the month of March, spring had arrived, and the snow had melted. As time went on, it became more and more difficult to find water. We tried to give what little we could scrounge to Livia and Ági. Most of the time, we exhausted ourselves walking the streets and searching the rubble for food and water. Jóska managed to trap a pigeon one day that we cooked on the wood stove in the apartment, using a chair for firewood.

"After all we've been through," Jóska exclaimed while the pigeon roasted, "for Hungary to fall to the Russians is an outrage. Why do you suppose the Americans didn't come?" He had not yet reconciled himself to our fate.

We ate that tough pigeon, our first meat in months, and it tasted delicious, so we started trapping pigeons as often as we could.

Jóska coughed all the time with a bad cold he couldn't shake. The children talked wistfully about various meals they remembered from before the war. I worried that they too were losing weight, though we felt we managed to keep them from going hungry.

The third day after we had moved into what we termed the pink palace, Jóska came home from an unsuccessful hunt for food. He reported that he had found a man who owned a boat and, for the remainder of our rice, would take us across the Danube. Aurél promised to get us a loaf of bread to take with us, but came up empty-handed.

Jóska obtained papers for us signed by a Mrs. Zsilinsky, the designated official in charge of Budapest, whose husband had been hanged by the Germans. The papers confirmed that we had been in the Resistance and were made out in Russian and Hungarian. We hoped these documents would allow us to get past the Russian soldiers patrolling the riverbanks, checking identifications, and keeping track of the people's movements.

The next morning, we bundled up our belongings and paused outside our newfound home, glancing back at the pink palace before heading for the Danube.

Àrpád, the man with the rowboat, met us as promised, and we piled into the boat. He pushed away from the bank and into the fast-moving current. Looking over the side of the boat, I realized to my horror that there were bodies of German soldiers, weighted down by rocks, on the bottom of the river.

"They were made to walk the plank," Àrpád said by way of explanation when he saw my horrified glance.

The water was unusually clear that spring, since no industries had been operating that winter to muddy up the waters with their waste. The expression on some of the faces of the corpses registered surprise. Others were contorted. I tried to distract the children by pointing at other boats farther downstream, but they too had seen the bodies and their attention was riveted to the sight.

As we neared the center of the Danube, it looked as if we were about to collide with a floating log. When Árpád pushed the log away with his oar, I realized it wasn't a log but a bloated body, floating on the surface. The man's eyes were open and mouth agape, as though forever screaming at the sky. I shuddered, and Jóska reached forward to pat my shoulder in an attempt to reassure me.

Livia and Ági seemed to accept these new and horrible sights without appearing to be upset. I thought about how much they had seen of war, destruction, and death during their young lives and wondered what their future would hold.

The boat bumped into the bank on the Pest side with a thud.

"Here we are, then. Watch your step," Árpád announced. He reached over to an iron ring protruding from the bank, to tie up his boat.

Russian soldiers, armed with submachine guns, awaited us at the top of the ladder leading to the street. They gestured to us to come up. The children scrambled up first, and the soldiers smiled and helped them. Then they helped Jóska with a backpack we had appropriated at the pink palace. It held all we had brought across. We planned to retrieve the suitcases that we had left with Aurél, if we decided to stay on the Pest side.

Soldiers of both the German and Russian armies were good to the children. The Germans had often given them bread and sometimes hot food from their field kitchen. This time, one of the soldiers, much to the children's delight, handed each a piece of cheese and said something in Russian.

Our papers passed inspection, and we headed for the apartment of some friends, hoping to find them home.

Though they took us in, they both were running fevers, so we only stayed the night and then moved on.

Next we spent two nights at the Wolfs. Clári Wolf was a cousin of mine. She and her husband Alfred had survived the war in hiding. Alfred had been a very wealthy banker before the war. When we entered their flat, incredible though it seemed, their servants were back in attendance. Some banking VIPs were being provided hot water for baths down one of the hallways. We did not qualify.

What seemed like a lifetime ago, before the siege, Jóska had been the director of the Agricultural Museum. Though no plan for governing the city had as yet been established by the Russians, and Jóska therefore had nowhere to go for information, we presumed he still had his job.

He walked with Livia to check out the museum buildings. They returned with the wonderful news that the director's flat was intact. Prior to the war, it had been occupied by Jóska's deputy, and now we could live there for the time being. We had no idea what had become of the deputy and his family.

Jóska found some of the staff from before the war, living on the museum grounds in various buildings. Everyone was scrambling for places to live, since most of Budapest had been bombed to rubble. We had hidden some food and clothing at the museum before the siege, but most of it had disappeared. Luckily, the museum was hooked up to an undamaged cistern, providing us with water, so we luxuriated in taking a bath the very first night.

Food was still scarce, but the museum staff gave us some of theirs, thus probably returning some of our stored supplies. The first Russian troops to arrive at the museum's shelter had raped all females, among them a four-year-old child and a seventy-five-year-old woman. Thank God, the girls and I had escaped such atrocities.

A few days after we settled in at the museum, my cousin Ágota appeared, having walked from Györ, a city near the Austrian border where she had survived the war with a group of people hiding at the local Catholic bishop's residence. She told us that the bishop had sheltered refugees, mostly women, some Jewish, some just afraid of the Russians. As the army had advanced, the first shockwave of Russian troops entered the bishop's cellar. He was down there as well, and heard some women screaming, among them his own niece's voice.

"Uncle Gabriel—help, help!"

The bishop, aware that his hour had struck, ran toward her.

"Get out!" he shouted at the soldiers.

One of the young Russians glanced at him and, pulling his gun, fired at the bishop from point-blank range.

Stunned silence descended on the cellar. Then people knelt, murmuring prayers. The bishop was placed on a stretcher. The young Russian who had shot him came over and, now appearing frightened, bent over His Excellency. The dying bishop raised his hand and blessed his assailant.

"I absolve you in the name of the Father and the Son and the Holy Ghost," he whispered.

"This is the most wonderful Good Friday of my life," he said to the young priests ministering to him as he took his last breath.

"No one else had thought of it—that it was Good Friday, in the Year of Our Lord 1945, when the bishop went to meet his Maker," Ágota concluded.

"It must be wonderful to have that kind of firm belief," I said. "My faith is in Jóska," I smiled at my husband. "He has been my rock through all this madness."

Jóska put his arm around my shoulder in an unusual public display of affection. In spite of my compliment, Jóska appeared to be very sad. I worried about him.

Among The Ashes

As the occupation wore on, a semblance of normalcy returned. The most brutal of the Russian troops rotated back to the Soviet Union. Units of military police were deployed throughout the city.

I did not quite realize how devastating the destruction of much of the museum must have been to Jóska. He had always treated his work in a rather humorous manner, but this may have been on the surface. I don't know.

A few days later, since he still wasn't feeling well, coughing worse, Jóska asked me to go back over to Buda to retrieve the suitcases. Although a pontoon bridge had been erected, he just wasn't up to making such a trip. He also wanted me to go to our burned-out apartment to try to find his signet and wedding rings in the rubble. He had taken them off the last time we had gone up to our apartment from the shelter, before the fire. I wanted to find the rings for Jóska's sake. On the other hand, my identity had gone up in smoke when I had burned my documents during the Nazi occupation. Had Jóska's aristocratic lineage also melted away with that signet ring, leaving us to start life anew?

I crossed the pontoon bridge, climbed the Buda hill, and noticed an eerie quiet. Where in times gone by there had been a steady chattering of birds, today there was no sound. They too had perished in the war. I walked up the Buda hill to the ruins of our apartment house and once again confronted the devastation that had been our home. I made my way to the fourth floor, watching out for missing steps and broken railings, and dug around among the ashes, sifting through my fingers what remained of our former life. *Vanished,* I thought, *those carefree days before the war - all gone.*

Though charred, the heavy support posts had withstood the fire. Some of the internal walls had burned or had been blasted away by the incendiary bomb, and I could not tell whether I was in the Denks' apartment across the hall or in our own, but the space around me overflowed with ghosts.

I stood beneath a gaping hole in the ceiling, glancing up at a clear blue sky. I waded through knee-high rubble. It would have taken weeks to sift through all of it. It distressed me that I couldn't find any sign of our wood-burning stoves or any other landmarks.

In the middle of it all stood a pink and blue china lamp minus the shade, unscathed. It had stood for many years on my bedside table. I thought of our neighbor who had carried a lampshade out of the fire. I wondered what had become of her. I felt cold and very much alone.

While I was rummaging through the charred remains of our lives, a fat black cat came from the direction of the Denks' apartment and followed me around, his fur gleaming in the rays of the afternoon sun in contrast with the ashes all around. He must have lived well on the mice and rats that roamed the remains of our devastated city. *Life would go on,* I thought, as I rubbed his ears. The tomcat licked my hand in return. I never found Jóska's rings and returned to the museum lugging only the blue lamp and the two suitcases I retrieved from Aurél on my way back.

We decided to place the girls in a convent boarding school that had reopened. Sacred Heart nuns, belonging to an order founded in France, operated the school and had managed to save some staples through the siege. They were in a better position to feed the children than we were. Jóska and I were both nonobservant Catholics, and Jóska particularly regarded religion akin to witchcraft. Though reluctant to have our daughters indoctrinated, we both felt the girls would be safer at the convent than roaming around the destroyed Agricultural Museum grounds. Unexploded grenades had injured children all over Budapest.

Jóska had Livia by the hand with Ági trailing behind as we pushed open the formidable carved front door of the convent.

Glossy, polished parquet floors contrasted with the devastation in the streets outside. We watched nuns glide soundlessly down the corridors. They reminded me of the black swans that used to inhabit the lake near the museum before the war. The sisters folded their arms into the long-flowing sleeves of their habits. Silver crosses hung around their necks, delicately bouncing on their chests.

"Was there no war here?" Livia whispered to Ági, who ignored her.

Groups of sailor-suited, uniform-clad girls in two straight lines followed in silence behind the gliding figures. Black stockings covered their young legs.

Mère (Mother) Pitzker welcomed the girls.

"Chiming bells control all waking hours: time to get up—one bell; time for Mass—two bells; time for breakfast—three; and so on, throughout the day. Wooden clackers are carried by all the teaching nuns. The sound of them must bring instant silence and assembly into two straight lines by all students. You'll catch on," she explained, trying to reassure Livia and Ági.

"Don't worry about uniforms, books, or tuition. We'll provide everything they need. Pay what you can, when you can," *Mère* Pitzker told us.

Jóska and I thanked her profusely, kissed Livia and Ági good-bye and left.

I did not like the finality with which the front door clanged shut behind us. The girls had looked scared and uncertain how to act in this strange new world. They had been told of unfamiliar rituals: curtsying to Reverend Mother; eating dinner in silence, while listening to Bible stories; washing themselves without taking off their underwear. I thought that was prudish, to say the least, and Jóska had rolled his eyes on hearing this particular rule.

The sound of vespers being sung in the chapel by otherworldly, clear, beautiful voices drifted through the windows, while Jóska and I walked away.

"Ironic, isn't it, that though we aren't believers," Jóska said on the way home, "each time we've needed help, it's come from the Catholic Church."

"Yes," I replied, thinking back to my days hiding at the legation.

"No matter how nice they are to the girls, I still think it's all nonsense." Jóska paused. "I just wish we didn't have to leave them." He appeared dejected, and I took his hand as we headed back towards the museum.

A few days later, one of the gardeners, Sándor, located us at the museum, having come from Cservölgy to bring us some most welcome apples and vegetables. Limited train service had by then been restored. Sándor told us that the house on the estate had been well taken care of; the Russians had come and gone without harming anything. It was the first news we'd had from there, so we were greatly relieved. I wanted to take the girls out of the convent and go back to Cservölgy with Sándor, but Jóska decided we should wait until he felt a little better.

We sent Sándor back to the farm. He had to jump off the train halfway home because a band of Soviet soldiers fired at it for no discernable reason. He ran for several kilometers and later caught another train to Veszprém, the closest town with rail service to Cservölgy. It was lucky for us we had not gone with him.

Our car, which had been stored at the museum, survived the war. We decided to have it turned into a pickup truck and to have the museum's logo painted on it. We hoped that as a business vehicle it would be less likely to be confiscated by the Russians, who showed a particular fondness for passenger cars. One afternoon, I walked to the garage to see how the conversion was progressing.

The garage owner gazed at me sadly. He told me that his establishment had been inspected by the authorities, and a soldier had commandeered our truck the minute he laid eyes on it.

When I returned to our apartment at the museum, Jóska wasn't there. His absence relieved me for a while of passing on the bad news. I spoke briefly with some workmen who were clearing rubble in front of the museum. One of them said Jóska had told them what needed to be done, and had implied he would be back later. He hadn't told the men where he was going, however.

As the day wore on and evening approached, I wondered where Jóska might be. I wished that telephone service had been restored, so that he could have contacted me.

Earlier in the day, when I had gone to see about the car, an old peasant woman had been sitting on the ground close to the garage. We had negotiated a trade. She had given me a scrawny chicken for a silver bracelet I had found in the ashes of our burned-out home. Now, while waiting for Jóska, I simmered the chicken with some onions the woman had thrown into the bargain. This would be the first time we had tasted chicken since before the siege had begun the previous fall. Chicken! *May 5, 1945, would be a red-letter day*, I thought.

I watched for Jóska through the window that overlooked the approach to the museum. The aroma from the pot on the stove was making me very hungry.

As six o'clock approached, I watched the workmen pack up their tools and settle their caps on their heads. Soon they departed through the museum gates. The sun was low on the horizon, and they needed to get home in daylight since the streets were still pockmarked with bomb craters and street lights had not yet been restored.

Still no Jóska. As twilight descended, I began to worry. *Where could he have gone? Perhaps he had stopped off to see Laci and Bebe,* I thought. *Maybe he was tracking down some food for us or supplies for the museum.* I hoped he wouldn't stay out past dark.

I poked the chicken with a fork and thought it was almost done. I glanced out the window one more time and saw Jóska entering the gate, some one hundred meters away. I quickly set the table, then threw open the apartment door to surprise him.

"We're having chicken!" I shouted.

To my dismay, an elderly stranger stood before me, not Jóska. He flipped open his wallet, which identified him as being Martin Biro, civilian, attached to a Russian clean-up brigade. Not many young men were left alive in Budapest, so old people had been conscripted to help the army secure war-damaged buildings all over the city. Mr. Biro twisted the cap in his hand.

"Ma'am, I don't know how to tell you this," he hesitated.

"What is it? Why are you here?" I asked, surprised at his formal tone of address. Weren't we all supposed to be comrades now?

"Your husband," Mr. Biro resumed speaking, "is dead, ma'am." Mr. Biro took a deep breath, then rushed on. "We found him in a building we were ordered to clear across town. He had fallen into a bomb crater."

Ability to function was taken from me. In my mind appeared a sharp image—the way Jóska had looked sitting on the veranda at Cservölgy, eating whipped cream cake. I felt the touch of his hand around my waist when we danced. A long thread of anguish coursed through my body, working its way into my heart, where it gripped me so that I could hardly breathe. I steadied myself against the door frame to keep from falling. I couldn't speak.

"Are you alone?" Mr. Biro asked. "Can I call someone for you?" he said, forgetting that the phones weren't working.

"I'll be all right," I stammered as the familiar black cloud descended and encircled me once again.

"This is where you go for information and to arrange for burial," Mr. Biro said, handing me a card. "They open at eight o'clock tomorrow." He hesitated a moment, and I heard his stomach growl. "Pardon me, ma'am, at a time like this," he stammered, "but where did you get the chicken?"

Jóska may be dead, but Mr. Biro had to eat. I walked over to the stove, picked up the pot and handed it to him, along with a potholder.

"Take it," I said. "There's no way I can eat now anyway."

He beamed at me, and forgetting his sad mission said "Bless you!" Then he was gone.

JÓSKA, JÓSKA, JÓSKA.

I could have lived with him for seventy instead of only seventeen years and would still not have known him fully. One thing, though, I did know: he had loved me.

My life was over.

May 6, 1945, the day after Jóska's death, dawned, wind rattling the museum windows. Following a sleepless night, my legs felt like lead when I willed myself to rise and face the day.

I walked to the office listed on the card Mr. Biro had given me and learned that Jóska had fallen from the seventh floor of one of the tallest buildings in the city into a shaft created by a bomb. No one we knew lived or worked there, nor could I think of any reason for Jóska to have gone to that building. More than likely, a bureaucrat informed me, Jóska had jumped and had not fallen. He had left no note, however, and there was no investigation by the authorities to confirm their suspicion. The coroner listed Jóska as a suicide. So many people had died, many taking their own lives, and so many were still buried in the rubble. What was one more death?

Jóska had seen our world crumble and our hopes for an American occupation dashed. Perhaps he had been unable to imagine his place in the future. In my relief that the fighting had ended and Hitler had been defeated, I had not realized the full extent of his hopelessness.

With Jóska's death, my world came to an end. In the next days, I couldn't understand why time was not standing still and why people around me were going on with their lives as though nothing had happened. Lines from a W. H. Auden poem kept going through my head:

"Stop all the clocks, cut off the telephone,
Prevent the dog from barking with a juicy bone,

Silence the pianos…"

But the clocks kept ticking, and the dogs continued barking. Music was irretrievably gone from my heart, from my hands, and my very soul. I knew that I would never play the piano again.

"He was my North, my South, my East and West,
My working week and my Sunday rest,
My noon, my midnight, my talk, my song;
I thought that life would last forever: I was Wrong."

No other words could better express how I felt when the realization that Jóska was dead struck me. I could envision no future—only a devastating loneliness. I wanted to close the drapes and shut out the light, lie down, go to sleep, and never wake up. Then, when I did go to bed, the last lines of the poem came to me unbidden:

"The stars are not wanted now: put out every one;
Pack up the moon and dismantle the sun;
Pour away the ocean and sweep up the wood;
For nothing now can ever come to any good."

I searched my mind for signs he might have given me.

"Now I could eat an entire whipped cream cake," Jóska had said to me the day before he died.

"Don't worry. It won't be long before we'll be drinking coffee with whipped cream on the veranda at Cservölgy once again," I had replied.

"The bastards will grab all the land. You'll see," Jóska had smiled at me and shaken his head. He had hated the occupation and felt a foreboding about the future.

Life as we had known it—the life of the Hungarian privileged class—was over for good. It had never occurred to me that he might have considered this a tragedy.

All through the siege there had not been a single angry word between us. We had even told each other that we were the only couple in our shelter who were not fighting. Tempers had flared among many.

Jóska had been coughing for months and suspected he might have had tuberculosis. There was no medical care available, so we had no diagnosis. Nor was there any penicillin to be had, if in fact he had the disease. Perhaps he wanted to spare my having to nurse him while trying to support the children. More than likely, he took his life for a combination of reasons, none of which gave me any comfort in my grief.

I delayed until late afternoon going to see our children at the Sacred Heart Convent School. I told myself that I was doing them a favor, giving them one more day without the knowledge of their father's death. In reality, I stalled because I did not know how to tell them.

"There is really nothing I can say that might comfort you. Maybe just that he was such a gentleman," one of the janitors said to me as I was leaving the museum. Word of Jóska's death had already managed to reach the workers. He was the sweetest, most good-natured person I had ever come across, and now he was dead.

I walked the couple of kilometers to the convent, trying to formulate the words, but my head pounded, and I felt sick to my stomach.

"Why, Jóska? Why, why, why? How could you?"

I managed to tell the nun who answered the door the reason I had come on a non-visiting day.

"God rest his soul," she murmured as she ushered me into Reverend Mother's parlor and told me to wait. Heavy medieval tapestries hung against the walls of the dimly lit room. The wind rattled the windows behind the maroon velvet drapes.

Can I get through this without breaking down? I wondered.

Mère Pitzker appeared, holding Livia and Ági by the hand. She gave me a sympathetic glance.

"Perhaps you'd like to take the girls out into Reverend Mother's garden," she said.

"Yes, thank you, Mother," I replied, rising.

The children looked puzzled because they knew they were not allowed in that garden, which was reserved for the head of the Sacred Heart nuns. I tried not to alarm them but couldn't keep my hands from shaking as I reached for theirs.

"Let's go sit outside."

"What's going on?" they asked in unison when we reached a secluded bench beneath a willow tree.

"Where is Papa?"

"Papa is dead," I said, tightening my grip on their hands.

There it was, the naked truth, and their childhood was over just like that.

"He can't be dead," Livia said. "He was here two days ago."

"He slipped and fell into a bomb crater in a building downtown," I said. I couldn't bring myself to tell them that he probably had jumped.

"How? What was he doing there?" Ági tried to ask.

"Shhhh," I told her. "We must be brave. Papa would want us to be."

Ági bit her lip, trying not to cry.

"But he was just here," Livia repeated. "He did a great imitation of *Mère* Pitzker gliding down the corridor. How could he be...?" She couldn't finish and burst into tears.

A gust of cold wind, a remnant of the past winter, blew through the garden, bending the branches of the willow under which we were sitting. I put my arms around my young daughters and held them close until they quieted.

"Do you know why the willow weeps, Mama?" Livia asked in a halting voice, looking up at the tree.

"No," I replied.

"*Mère* Pitzker says it's because the cross on which Christ died was made from a willow and that no willow has stood up straight since that time."

"Do you think that's true?" Ági asked, skepticism in her voice.

So like her father, I thought. *Don't believe everything they tell you,* I wanted to say. The religious teachings were myths in my opinion, but I felt uneasy contradicting the nuns about such matters, so I thought for a moment before replying. "Notice how it bends but does not break."

The girls seemed to understand that I was talking about the three of us, not the willow.

We rose from the bench and walked back down the garden path, then went inside.

"I'll be back at visiting time, after the funeral tomorrow," I told them.

"Can't we come with you?" Livia pleaded.

"No, funerals are too sad for children. Papa would want you to be happy, not sad," I replied.

We walked along the school corridor toward the front door. It was beginning to rain, and when I opened the heavy wooden door to leave, Livia and Ági clung to me.

"You must be brave," I told them again. I kissed them good-bye and slowly extricated myself from their arms. Leaving my girls standing in the doorway, I walked out into the rain.

Jóska's body was cremated the next day in compliance with Russian regulations; then interred. A priest, who had conducted too many funerals, said a few words. Nothing he said or did allayed the colossal ache in my heart.

My parents had survived and were still living at Alice Mercer's since their house had sustained a direct hit and there were no apartments to be had.

When school let out in June, my parents, the girls, and I retraced our journey of what seemed like a thousand years ago, before the war: we took the train to the farm at Cservölgy. Wildflowers bloomed among the weeds growing beside the railroad tracks. We passed through a burned forest.

"Papa, will the trees grow green again?" Ági asked, turning toward me. She covered her mouth with both hands.

"I keep forgetting, sorry." She reached over and patted my hand. I wished that I could bring myself to tell our daughters how much I too missed Jóska. I was afraid I'd fall apart if I did, so I tried not to talk about him at all.

Forever Alone

Having to work helped me to survive those first months after Jóska's death. The children outgrew the few things they had and needed new clothes and shoes. It was up to me to do something about this.

Much as I had loathed my English governesses when I was a child, the lessons they had taught me now became my lifesaver. I passed a proficiency test and was hired by the Proletarian Language Institute to teach English classes that the Russians had established. Since people all over the country were scheming to get out of Hungary, many dreaming of going to America, English lessons were in great demand.

Problems began cropping up at Cservölgy. Jóska had managed the farm, and I knew little about crops or animals; nor was I used to being the boss. My father was supposed to be running things, but his health had deteriorated during the war, and he wasn't coping too well. The children were under my mother's care during their summer vacation, and I had to be in Budapest to teach. The girls' antics were a bit much for Mother, but both my parents did their best to help me.

In the midst of the work, wartime memories came unbidden into my mind. Jóska's presence remained, and the feeling persisted that I truly had everything during those seventeen years the two of us had spent together. He had a gift for turning even plain, ordinary Mondays into something special—always full of life and fun and plans.

Snippets of our life together came to my consciousness day and night. I recalled our walking in companionable silence through ankle-deep autumn leaves in the woods at Cservölgy, leaves crackling underfoot and migrating geese honking farewell as they flew in V formation overhead.

I remembered late one winter afternoon, riding in a horse-drawn sleigh back to Cservölgy where we had come to spend the children's Christmas holidays. The horses were softly neighing ahead of us. The snow-laden branches of the oak trees that lined the road bowed overhead, forming the nave of a cathedral. We rounded a curve in the road and saw the lights of our house down in the valley. Jóska took my hand in his very carefully so the coachman wouldn't see. It wouldn't do to display affection! I knew he had the same picture in his mind as I had: two poppy-cheeked little girls in their flannel pajamas, eating their supper in the dining room with the fire crackling.

I recalled too, far back in time, several years before we were married, a ski trip in the Buda hills. Heavy fog had rolled in, and he had told me that we were lost. He didn't realize that I would have been happy to remain lost with him forever.

Jóska's real home had been Cservölgy. He loved the place and really had belonged there. After he died, I would catch myself expecting him to step out of the woods, assorted dogs and two little girls at his heels.

I smiled when I thought of the dogs Jóska had named after the minister of education and other notables—this at a time when his father was the chief inspector of education. My father had been very upset and worried when he learned what Jóska had done, for fear that Jóska would land in trouble. Jóska never had the slightest intention of kowtowing to authorities or the privileged, however, and he managed to get away with such antics.

Moments of utter desolation overwhelmed me from time to time. In late June, after teaching English all week in Budapest, I caught the night train to Cservölgy for the weekend. It was after ten o'clock when the train arrived in Veszprém, the nearest stop. Since the town was still under a nine o'clock curfew, most people were obliged to spend the night at the station.

Before leaving Budapest that afternoon, I had wanted to tell our friends Bebe and Laci about Jóska's death. When I had gone by their apartment, Laci told me that Bebe was visiting her sister Magdi in Veszprém. Magdi lived across town from the depot. I thought I'd try to reach her house to spend the night in spite of the curfew. I walked from the station into the empty moonlit streets, feeling utterly alone. I wondered whether the Russian patrols would shoot on sight or just stop me. I didn't care. I traversed the length of the town to Magdi's house and saw not one soul on the way.

I knocked on the front door, and Bebe answered. She threw her arms around me in absolute delight to see a familiar face.

"Jóska is dead," I blurted out.

Bebe's face contorted in grief. Unable to speak, she took my hand and led me into the living room. Logs burned in a blue-tiled fireplace. For a moment, the only sounds were of sparks and crackling of the disintegrating wood. Bebe pulled me down onto the couch beside her and looked at me, her eyes brimming with tears. The numbness and isolation I had felt ever since Jóska's death erupted, and I found myself sobbing. We talked and cried through the night.

The next day, a local man gave me a ride in his cart as far as the Cservölgy road. Wildflowers were blooming, fruit trees had burst into blossom, birds were singing, and the sky was a stunning blue.

Don't the flowers, the trees and the birds know that Jóska is dead?

The farm's remote location had kept all but a handful of Russians from venturing near, and uninterrupted, our workers had planted and harvested crops during the war.

The house, although broken into by locals or stray Russian troops, was intact, save for a missing radio, Jóska's shaving gear, and my bathrobe.

While I had been working in the city, my father had taken things in hand. Unfortunately, Apu had fired Sándor, who had been doing a good job and had exhibited great loyalty by risking the dangerous journey to Budapest to bring us food and the good news that the house at Cservölgy had survived the war. Apu meant well, of course: he had let Sándor go as an economic measure. My father, however, insisted on doing such things without consulting me or anybody else. Though I tried to find Sándor to remedy the situation, he had vanished.

I continued teaching English in Budapest and going to Cservölgy for weekends. Most of my salary had to be used to keep the farm afloat until the harvest in late summer when the crops could be sold. Properties all around us were confiscated by the state and turned into collectives. That summer, however, we received an exemption on our farm because of Jóska's part in the Resistance. For the moment at least, we could remain on the farm and keep it operating.

Since most of Budapest had been bombed to rubble, housing was in extremely short supply. Bebe and Laci were thrilled to find a vacant apartment, intact except for still boarded-up windows. They used a wheelbarrow to move what was left of their belongings to their new home. After they settled into it, they learned that the flat had belonged to a couple who had killed themselves on their way to the West. Though people longed to escape the Russian occupation, many despaired when faced with leaving home and family behind.

I too was traveling light. The sole surviving lamp from our apartment had been stolen from a garage where some friends had let me store it. My one suit was swiped from the cleaners.

On the other hand, I was making more money than any of my male friends at the time. The demand for English lessons kept rising. People were willing to sell their meager possessions to sign up for classes. I realized how lucky I was compared to many who had no salable skills.

Many wanted to share in my good fortune. Jóska's brother Feri trekked across the pontoon bridge on the Danube to see me. He wanted to know whether I would lend him enough so that he could haul his piano from one place to another. It was only slightly comic that Feri should come and make such an outrageous request of his newly widowed sister-in-law. I did, in fact, lend him the money, and he eventually paid it back, but he had no notion of how hard I struggled to keep body and soul together and the girls fed and clothed.

In our postwar world, the women generally functioned better than the men. Juci, Jóska's only sister, exemplified this. She, like me, had never worked. Within days of the end of the war, however, she found a job running the buffet at the Budapest Opera House, which had miraculously escaped the bombing. The Russians believed in bread and circuses, and they wanted the opera to reopen early in the city's clean-up operations.

I dropped by to see Juci at work. I caught sight of her, bustling around in the tiny space behind the counter, her hair as blond as ever, beautifully coiffed, a tribute to the beauty parlors that had reopened within days of the guns having been stilled. Juci was wearing a frilly, spanking-clean blouse made of white parachute silk and a ragged skirt, a none-too-clean half-apron, and very worn felt slippers.

"Juci," I asked, "What in the world—why do you look like this?"

"Dearie," she replied with a wide smile, "what doesn't show over the counter is not important right now."

She offered me a room in her apartment. I promptly accepted as I had been moving around and staying with friends, since I had no right to stay at the museum after Jóska's death.

Steven

In late summer, I was hired as editor of the English version of the largest Hungarian weekly, our only outlet to the West. The publisher warned me to allow nothing to be printed that the Russian censors would disapprove of, and I took him seriously. Nonetheless, a few weeks later, as relations between East and West deteriorated, the newspaper was suspended.

Before long, I found a job doing translations for the British-Hungarian Society, a cultural organization. In the afternoons and evenings, I continued to teach English classes. I had little talent for teaching and didn't enjoy the work. The demand was such, however, that it didn't seem to matter whether I was a good teacher or not. In fact, my classes were very popular.

During the fall of 1946, I taught a class of fifty advanced students. At the end of one week's session, I assigned them a difficult translation. Among the papers handed in during our next class meeting, I found an outstanding one.

"Which one of you is Colonel Molnár?" I asked the class. No one responded. Molnár was absent that night. I read his translation to the class, and all the students were impressed. The following week Colonel Molnár returned to class and afterward talked with me. He seemed proud of his English achievement.

Steven Molnár looked middle-aged; he had a medium build and penetrating blue eyes. I sensed that he understood life and me very well. I can't quite explain it, but I also felt that there were dark and terrible places in his heart.

Colonel Molnár lived quite close to Juci's apartment, and he suggested that we walk toward our homes together. Since I knew Juci was at work and we could have her apartment to ourselves, I invited Steven in for a cup of tea.

As we talked, I came to realize that he was the same person

we had heard about during the war, the man who had rescued two women from one of the ghetto houses and refused to take the loyalty oath to the Nazi Party leader.

"I organized a partisan battalion to fight both the Nazis and the Russians," Steven related, while stoking the wood-burning stove so that I could boil water for our tea. "We sabotaged the German war effort, trying to keep them from blowing up rail lines and bridges. We also sabotaged the Russians, with the hope that the American armies would advance and occupy Hungary when the war was over." I handed Steven a steaming mug and sat down across the table from him to listen.

"When the Russians overtook our battalion, I joined forces with their advancing army and came marching into Budapest with the Russian troops. At first, the Russians thought that I was on their side. Then they realized that I had been parachuted in to take charge of Ukrainian partisans. That was the end of my pretended romance with the Russians," he chuckled. "I went to prison for several months."

"How dreadful for you," I interjected, but Steven went on with his story, as though I hadn't spoken.

"One night, they made me dig my own grave. I thought I'd be executed in the morning." Steven said all this as though he were relating the weather report. I marveled at his courage.

"Then the Russians released me," he leaned toward me, "with no reason given. They put me in command of a Hungarian battalion about to be demobilized. Some weeks later, without explanation, they arrested me again and threw me in prison for two more months of interrogation.

"Among other methods of torture, a dentist drilled into my healthy teeth without anesthetic." I gasped when he said this. Beads of perspiration formed on Steven's forehead. He looked at me but seemed oblivious of his own or my distress and continued.

"Another night, my inquisitors attached electrodes to my genitals and nipples and gave me electric shocks until I passed out."

Steven kept on talking as though a floodgate had opened. He told me that as a Hungarian officer, he had ordered similar tortures to be inflicted on Russian and German prisoners in the Ukraine. He ended his story by telling me that he had once again been released and returned to active duty.

Steven stopped by one Sunday afternoon a few weeks later. He had been to lunch at the American consulate.

"Do you think that's a healthy thing for you to do?" I asked him. He shrugged his shoulders.

"Do you think the Russians will arrest me a third time?"

"I don't think so," I said, "since things seem to be returning to some semblance of normalcy. But then again that may be wishful thinking."

One evening in November 1946, I worked late in my classroom, correcting papers. A young girl, perhaps nineteen, knocked and entered. She looked very pale and shaky, which was not unusual in those days. She introduced herself as Márta Tott. When I asked her what she wanted, she began to cry.

"I'm not sure I can trust you," she sobbed.

"So then don't talk to me," I answered.

A hysterical woman, whom I had never met, was all I needed.

"I have a message from Steven Molnár," she said, drying her tears. "He received a warning that he is about to be arrested a third time. He climbed out through his kitchen window to avoid the police. He's staying with my family in the country."

"What's that to do with me?" I asked, not knowing whether to trust the girl.

"He needs false papers and cash to get across the border into the American-occupied sector of Austria. He wants to know if you can help. He'd sign his apartment over to you," Márta concluded.

I thought for a minute. Needless to say, I wanted no part of his apartment in such a situation. Any aid I might render could not be paid for.

"Call me in the morning and I'll have an answer for you," I said, needing time to think.

I lay awake most of the night and wondered what Jóska would have me do. I had a whole set of Jóska's documents—perfect for clearing any checkpoints. Most had no photos on them, and on others it would not be too hard to substitute Steven's picture. I wondered whether I had the right to take the risk. If Steven were to be found out, the documents would lead straight to me. Were I to be arrested, could my parents manage to cope with the children?

I decided that Jóska, in view of Steven's background as a Resistance fighter, would do what he could, and so would I.

I did not want to give an unknown girl the papers, however. I called Márta and told her I would go with her the next day to hand them to Steven myself at his hiding place. She hesitated but agreed to come for me. In the morning, Márta fetched me in an old, beat-up pickup truck and drove me to a farm about twenty kilometers outside the city. Both of us kept a sharp lookout, but no one seemed to be following us. When we arrived at our destination, Márta directed me to a barn. Steven stepped out from behind some bundles of straw. Without preamble, I handed him the documents, wanting to spend as little time with him as possible to lessen the danger of being seen.

"As far as I know," I told him, "the border has been closed completely for several days. One of my students had to turn back two days ago. If you can't get out, you can stay at Cservölgy. It's out of the way. Nobody would think to look for you there."

"If I can't get across, I will meet you at the Veszprém bus stop next Saturday." As I turned to leave, he put his hand on my arm and said, "By the way, Éva, thank you."

"There is no need," I replied.

Márta had not switched off the truck's engine. I climbed in, and she drove me back to Budapest.

The Tott family, which was harboring Steven, felt uneasy because I might have been seen. They were afraid to keep him at their house any longer. He hid in open fields for several days. Not many people moved around the countryside at that time, so he remained undetected. I felt I had to help Steven find another safe haven.

Snow fell, obliterating the landscape as my bus pulled into the depot at Veszprém that Saturday evening. I looked out the window, straining to see Steven. I spotted him dressed in a heavy overcoat and cap, standing so that he was partially hidden by a pillar inside the station.

"I was afraid to try for the border without a guide," Steven explained.

"Come with me," I replied and led him to the bus that would take us to the road leading to Cservölgy.

How would I explain Steven's presence to my parents?

Whatever I told them, they would assume romantic involvement. Apu and Mother could not envisage my going it alone, raising the girls. I decided I would let my parents think what they would and make no explanations, except that Steven needed help. Since Jóska's death, I felt emotionally dead, and Steven seemed to understand that.

When I introduced him to my parents, knowing looks passed between them, but they asked no questions and made Steven welcome.

Steven had a quick mind. In short order, he realized the farm was floundering under my father's care. Although he had never had anything to do with farming, Steven set about studying Jóska's books on orchards, animal husbandry, and the like. My father gladly relinquished the reins, though he played the reluctant debutante for a while.

I introduced Steven as the new overseer to the workers, and they did not seem to question his presence at the big house. He had a set of false papers, other than the ones I had taken to him, and since the farm was remote, with few visitors, he seemed to be safe for the moment.

Toward the end of summer, Steven oversaw the shipment to market of the first postwar fruit harvest. That autumn, we had a positive cash flow at Cservölgy once again.

Steven and I both knew the long-term solution to his problem would be to leave Hungary, and that we were just delaying the inevitable.

I carried messages from Steven to Walter Maher, who at the time was a vice consul at the American embassy in Budapest. Steven's partisan division had been in touch with the Americans during the war, giving them information on Russian and German troop movements, so the Americans owed him a favor. Various schemes were proposed by Maher to get Steven out of the country.

One day, Maher drove to Cservölgy, causing much excitement among our workers, since he arrived in an embassy vehicle. I chided the vice consul and suggested that if he planned to come again, to please use less conspicuous transportation. It was a miracle that he did not lead the authorities straight to Steven.

The next time Maher came to see Steven in a red school bus. Maher, a silver spoon, had sat out the war as a 4-F, for some reason physically unfit for military service. He obviously did not understand the precariousness of our situation.

All of us felt extremely nervous for several days after Maher's visit, fearing that someone would look into why he was visiting Cservölgy. Walter Maher had come to debrief Steven about some of his wartime activities in the Ukraine and to supply him with names of contacts in Vienna.

After much discussion, I tentatively decided that it would be best for the girls if the three of us also were to attempt to leave the country. If we could escape, Livia and Ági could grow up somewhere in the West, instead of in Soviet-occupied Hungary.

The discussions about whether, when, and how to leave were interminable. One evening, Steven and I were sitting in the library after the girls had gone to bed.

"I don't want to go unless it becomes absolutely necessary," Steven said.

"You are not being realistic," I replied. "How long do you think you can stay here before someone becomes suspicious and informs on you? Besides, what kind of a life can you foresee for any of us, considering the inflation?"

Economic conditions were incredibly difficult, inflation was rampant, and there was no improvement in sight.

"I know all that, but I still don't want to go unless I have to."

"I've been taking my pay in cash every night, so I can spend it before the shops close. Otherwise the money becomes worthless by morning," I told him. "I cart my daily earnings in a shopping bag. No one knows the denominations except by color. The government just keeps printing money. How long can that go on?

"I've heard that the Red Cross is taking children to Switzerland for vacations. Perhaps the girls could go, and we could cross the border into Austria while they are out there," I told him.

A shuffling sound came from the top of the stairs, and I realized that the girls had been eavesdropping.

I climbed the stairs to their bedroom, but the children had scampered back to bed and were pretending to be asleep. *They know what's going on,* I thought; *there's no need for explanations.* I kissed them both and, unburdened of the need to tell them of our plan, retraced my steps.

Steven talked about our future. He had been a partisan for too long and had endured too many things to trust anyone completely, even me. I had lived through persecution and the loss of my other self when Jóska died. Although we had become friends of sorts, Steven and I had no romantic illusions. We agreed that we would marry before crossing the border, so that if something happened to me during the journey, he would have legal claim to Livia and Ági and could make decisions about their future. We planned to inform my parents before leaving Cservölgy.

In the midst of all the anxiety of planning, a letter came from Borcsa *néni*'s sister, telling me that Borcsa *néni* had died in her sleep. I had thought myself drained of all emotion by Jóska's death, but I was wrong. Borcsa *néni*'s passing devastated me all over again. I made an inadequate stab at informing the girls, who seemed to take the news calmly.

Later that day, though, I looked out the kitchen window and saw Livia and Ági conducting a funeral under an oak tree. They were pretending that a matchbox was a casket. Before the war, the children had often buried insects in this way and imitated mourners they had read about in books. This time, when they placed the little box into the ground, both of them were sobbing. *I must try to make a whipped cream cake for them sometime soon,* I thought.

Within a few days, I made arrangements to place the children with two Swiss families. The Red Cross official in charge of their files told me that it would be impossible for Livia and Ági to go to the same household, because no one wanted to take on two children. I consoled myself with the fact that the two host families were related and had assured the Red Cross that the girls would see each other from time to time. Ági would be placed with the Braun family, and Livia with the Brauns' adult daughter and son-in-law, the Freys.

The next weekend I told the girls that I would be taking them to Budapest on Monday to prepare for the trip. They talked me into staying "just one more night" at Cservölgy, and I could hear them creeping around after everyone was in bed.

When I went to investigate, I found them barefoot standing

in their nightgowns, in the doorway of the living room. Moonlight lit up the veranda and illuminated the rooms, interspersed with shadows. The children gazed at Jóska's study, now taken over by Steven. Here they had pored over the horse breeding books a few days earlier, trying to figure out how babies were made.

I watched them from the doorway and realized that they were bidding good-bye to the places they loved. The girls glanced into the dining room where so many friends had eaten and family celebrations taken place. I thought of the incident when Ági had told András to take his elbows off the table, and I smiled.

I followed as Livia and Ági tiptoed to the kitchen where Borcsa *néni* used to produce all sorts of wonders. I knew the children must be thinking of her.

The moonlight exaggerated the high ceilings and the graceful arches leading to the veranda. Livia turned and saw me. She looked a bit frightened at being discovered, but when she saw that I wasn't angry, she said, "Ours is the most beautiful house in the world, and we will never see it again, will we, Mama?" Not expecting an answer, she took Ági by the hand and led her up the stairs to their bedroom.

The sun had not yet risen and the silence on the farm was complete when I woke the girls. They heard me enter their room and burrowed their heads under their pillows.

"Kis *bácsi* (the old coachman) is waiting with the carriage. Hurry up, girls." They slowly, reluctantly, dressed and prepared themselves, ready to go.

My parents stood in their bathrobes outside the big front door, waiting to say good-bye.

"We'll see you in a few months," Apu said as he hugged the girls. He had tears in his eyes.

"Live well, my child," I heard him whisper to Ági when he let go of her hand.

As the carriage pulled away to take us to the train at Veszprém,

Mother and Apu waved until the carriage rounded the corner out of the driveway, and the girls waved back.

Arrangements were complicated because the host families for the two girls lived in different towns. Livia was assigned to travel by train to Switzerland, and Ági was to fly. Ági and I took Livia to the train. Though she tried hard to act the part of the tough, older sister, tears trickled down her cheeks. She pressed her nose against the window of her compartment, for a last glimpse of us standing on the platform. Though I felt like crying myself, I smiled and waved until the train was out of sight, trying to reassure her.

The next day was Ági's turn. I had sewn ten gold Krugerrands into her teddy bear the night before. I had explained to her that we needed to try to get some money out of the country.

"If Customs asks, tell them a woman at the airport handed you the bear to give to someone meeting the plane in Zurich. You don't remember her name," I told her.

"Don't worry, Mama," Ági said, pulling herself up to her full four-foot-four-inch height, "I'll sneak it past them."

Inside each girl's shoe, I tucked letters, written in French by the nuns at the convent where they had been in school. French is the international language of the Sacred Heart order. Addressed to any Sacred Heart convent, anywhere in the world, the letters instructed that the nuns provide for the children, should they show up on their doorstep.

"Just in case," I had told Livia and Ági, dreading that they might ask, "Just in case of what?" They accepted my explanation without comment. At least, if Steven and I were both killed crossing the border, Livia and Ági would have someplace to go.

At the airport, we hugged and kissed, but Ági seemed preoccupied as we approached Customs. I was directed by an official to stay in a cordoned area, while Ági approached the table where an agent was seated. She held the little golden bear under one arm and carried her small, gray cardboard suitcase in her other hand.

As she reached the table, I saw her glance down at her feet. It seemed a deliberate gesture and had the desired effect. The customs official also looked at her feet. I noticed that she was wearing one white-and-green-striped sock and one red one, the colors of Hungary's flag.

"Colorblind and left-footed," I heard her say, as she grinned at the agent. He laughed in spite of himself.

The little rascal is trying to take his attention off that bear, I thought. The man said something to her and Ági tried to swing her suitcase up onto the table with one hand, while hanging on to her bear with the other, without much success.

The inspector stepped around the table and lifted the bag for her. He opened it, and while his hands felt around the sides of the suitcase, his eyes peered over the top and regarded Ági. She looked unconcerned, but the agent's eyes narrowed as his glance fell on the gold-laden bear. Without a word, his hand reached over the table and pointed at the bear.

Should I step forward? What have I done, involving a child in such an errand? What will they do to her if they find the gold? Oh, God! What could I do to divert attention? But I stood silently, gripping the rope separating me from my daughter. Ági handed over the bear, with what appeared to me to be utter panache. The agent held the little bear in his big gruff hands as though weighing it.

"What's inside, little lady?" he inquired.

"Cotton or straw, I guess," Ági squeaked in response. Her voice wasn't her own. I hoped the agent wouldn't know the difference.

"It feels heavy," the inspector said. I shuddered, but couldn't think what to do to help.

"Why don't you cut it open, if you don't believe me?" I heard Ági say with all the authority in her voice that she could muster. The expression on her face mirrored Jóska's when speaking to one of the workers on the farm.

I realized that my ten-year-old daughter was trying to bluff her way through the situation by acting indignant. I held my breath while the hardened agent glared at her. Their eyes locked, but Ági didn't blink.

"All right," he said, after what seemed like an eternity. He handed back the bear and shut the suitcase. "You can go."

Ági took the suitcase, turned her head, and winked at me with Jóska's unmistakable insolence, then walked toward the departure gate. *This child will be all right, whatever happens,* I thought, and was comforted.

By Christmas 1947, Livia and Ági had been in Switzerland for three months. The holiday seemed empty without them. I longed to see them. Steven and I decided to leave the country as soon as possible. Apu, upset over our plans, refused to accept the idea that the government would soon take the farm away from us. The laws changed daily, and more and more property was being confiscated. It was becoming clear that the Soviets planned to collectivize the entire country.

I had been offered a position as head of the English Department in the ministry of education, but in that kind of Western oriented job, one did not last long before the knock on the door came. I had been promoted to office manager of the British-Hungarian Society, which was bad enough. I had no desire to become a political prisoner. My counterpart at the American-Hungarian Society, with whom I shared an office, warned me that detectives were watching his house.

My father wanted me to let Steven leave the country by himself. *The sooner the better,* he must have thought, although he didn't say so. Apu hoped against hope that we could return to our prewar lifestyle, if only Steven's presence were removed from our midst.

Many of our friends, Bebe and Laci among them, had crossed the border by this time, headed for a new life somewhere around the globe. I asked my father whether he seriously suggested that I have the children brought back from Switzerland. Without hesitation, he gave his one-word reply. "Yes."

"On your head be it, if anything happens to them!" I shouted at him.

I thought for a moment that he was going to hit me. Later, I heard from many friends that such scenes were taking place in most families when the younger generation talked about leaving. Apu doubtless felt that if we left, our parting would be forever.

Steven called me at work one morning in January to tell me that my father had died quite unexpectedly of an aneurysm. In my heart, I knew that Apu had died many months earlier, perhaps when I first saw him wearing the Star of David during the war. The man I knew as my father had not existed after that time. My all-powerful father, on whom the sun rose and set, had vanished, along with so much else, under the heels of the Nazis.

Tears streamed down my face as I continued my telephone conversation with Steven.

"Do you want him buried in Veszprém or Cservölgy?" Steven asked. Veszprém had the nearest cemetery.

"I think at Veszprém. Cservölgy won't last much longer in private hands, and I don't want Apu resting forever on a Soviet collective."

Mother decided, however, that in spite of the risk of the unknown future of our land, Apu should be put to rest at Cservölgy. Perhaps her grief affected her judgment. I didn't argue with her.

We buried him on a gusty winter day on a knoll in the almond orchard where he had loved to stroll in the springtime. Mother and I hoped that his grave would remain undisturbed. A marble slab marked the spot, giving only the dates of his birth and death and the simple word "Anonymous," per Apu's instructions.

Even though she was in good health, I worried about my mother now that she was widowed. She knew of Steven's and my plans to leave Hungary but insisted she could manage on her own. I found her a room in Budapest in one of the few homes left standing in her old neighborhood. She crammed what seemed to me to be half of Cservölgy into that one room and announced that she too would become a working woman.

Mother had traveled many times to England, sometimes staying months at a time, and was fluent in English. From an editor friend, she managed to secure some work she could do at home, translating English periodicals into Hungarian. Apu had known many people in the publishing field, and Mother had no lack of sources. During the next couple of years, she undertook the translation of John Gunther's *Inside USA*. She scoffed at the notion that she might be arrested if anyone found out, since the book had been banned and smuggled into Hungary.

Steven and I decided to leave and to try to get Mother out of the country later if she wanted to join us. She could probably obtain a passport considering her age.

I went to Budapest for two days before we left. It felt strange to know I was leaving and probably seeing every place and everybody for the last time.

Jóska's sister Juci, unaware of our plans, parted from me casually.

"See you next Wednesday," she said, referring to our habit of lunching together on that day. I looked back as she walked away, to catch a glimpse of her for the last time.

That evening, I stopped by to see Alice Mercer. When I confided in her that I planned to leave the country, she promised to keep an eye on my mother.

"You are leaving with a man who speaks little English?" Alice questioned me. "What do you have to offer if you ever get to Canada, Australia or America?"

"My English is very good."

"So, 200 million people in America speak good English. What else?"

"A better-than-average knowledge of people."

"Well, that's something. What else?"

"A really nice pair of legs?" I raised my skirt a bit and turned my ankle in her direction without much enthusiasm.

She laughed. It was not a happy laugh.

My last day at work came. A major in the police force, one of my star pupils, followed me into the office after class.

"I hear the border is closed again. I was going to try this week. Have you heard anything?" He was either a spy for the government or was taking a big risk talking to me.

I looked at him for a moment. With good instincts, I considered myself a fair judge of people, so I took a chance and leveled with him.

"I'm in a hurry to get home. It's snowing." I said, gathering my handbag and coat. "Walk with me," I invited, not wanting to talk within earshot of coworkers.

"My fiancé and I are going to try," I told him when we reached the street. "If I'm not back on Friday and you don't hear of my arrest, it means we made it."

"So, you are engaged," he said. "Well, I'm glad you are not going alone. I wish I'd met you earlier."

I promised to send him all my English textbooks and told him to be very careful before deciding what to do. By this time we had reached the corner where our routes diverged, and he said good-bye. The temperature had risen, and the earlier snowfall had turned to sleet.

Before returning home, I decided to go to the cemetery to say good-bye to Jóska. If I could turn my back and walk away from there, maybe I could do anything. The snow was deep and the shadows cast by the lampposts were long across the graves.

"Until we meet again," I whispered and trudged towards the cemetery gates to face alone what seemed to me an interminable future.

Steven and I left that night for Szombathely (Saturday Place), a town near the Austrian border. Jews had gathered there through the centuries, coming in from the surrounding countryside for the Sabbath. *An appropriate departure point,* I thought, but kept it to myself.

We both carried cyanide capsules, which I had obtained on my last day in Budapest on Steven's instructions. Alice Mercer had some left over from the time of the Nazi occupation and had given them to me.

I had handed one to Steven quite casually.

"Oh, and here's the cyanide you wanted," I told him.

The fact that he was taken aback showed me he had not moved in Jewish circles during the war. Just about everyone in hiding and those harboring them had acquired some. I kept one pill for myself.

Steven and I took the train, carrying backpacks to blend in with weekend hikers headed for that region. We stuffed our small suitcases under the seat. No one paid any attention to us. At one point between two villages, we were alone in our compartment.

"If anything happens to me, promise you'll take care of the girls," I said to Steven.

"Marry me now, Éva, so I'll have some claim to them."

I had kept putting off marrying him; the thought of it gave me a hollow feeling inside. I knew the time had come, however, so I agreed.

As the train pulled into Szombathely, we spotted a bombed-out church on a side street. The adjacent rectory was still standing, and we knocked on the door. A rather dour, elderly priest opened it. He seemed to understand that we were border-crossers, though our plans remained unspoken, and was willing to perform the ceremony.

With a crude crucifix staring down at us from the sacristy

wall, the priest married us. His housekeeper acted as witness. This desolate setting was so very different from the beautiful chapel where my marriage to Jóska had taken place.

As we walked from the church toward a nondescript hotel, Steven noticed a Russian soldier standing in a doorway, lighting a cigarette. The young man looked like any other soldier to me.

"I don't like the looks of him. Let's step into that inn across the road," Steven said, frowning. We cut across the street and entered through a tavern door. Steven asked the proprietor if we could use the restroom to wash up before we ate. The man motioned down a corridor. We piled our belongings outside the restroom doors and entered separate facilities. I knew that Steven, after years of intelligence service, had a nose for trouble. I suspected he wanted an opportunity to jettison the directions to the meeting place our guide had sent him.

When we came out of the bathrooms, we went to sit in the pub and ordered lunch. Steven eyed the street through a nearby window.

"Sir, a soldier followed you in here," the proprietor said, addressing Steven in a low voice. "I think you should know he went through your knapsacks. Said he was searching for weapons."

"Thanks for telling us," Steven said to our host, handing the man a tip as he rose; he motioned me to follow.

"Back to Cservölgy at once," he said, helping me put on my backpack with one hand while handing me my suitcase. He threw his own pack over his shoulder, grabbed my hand, and led me back out the door toward the train station. I dreaded the thought of being caught and glanced up and down the street for any sign of pursuit. Steven, outwardly at least, seemed completely calm. I felt him to be in complete control of the situation.

During our attempt to get close to the border and our subsequent border crossing, Steven proved to be a real professional with enormous courage and the capacity for decision making that set him apart from any civilian I knew. We returned to the farm and resumed our lives as though we had been away hiking over the weekend. We waited until our contact man sent word once again that the time was right to attempt to get across.

I kept the cyanide capsule in my pocket along with my new marriage certificate.

Through The Iron Curtain

My mother had mixed feelings about Steven and me having married. She'd been very fond of Jóska and thought Steven to be a poor replacement. On the other hand, she felt I needed taking care of, particularly if we went through with what she considered to be an idiotic plan to leave the country.

I wrote to the girls in Switzerland and explained that no man would ever take the place of their father. I could not, of course, tell them the real reason that I married Steven—that I did not want them stranded in Switzerland or sent back to Hungary if I should die while attempting to cross the border. I hoped they would have a new life, preferably in America. Both girls wrote, congratulating us in cool tones. Livia asked not too subtle questions about our bedroom arrangements at Cservölgy. It was evident to me that my daughters did not want a stepfather. In my next letter to Livia, I assured her that Steven continued to sleep in Jóska's study.

Steven was a good man, but I couldn't help comparing his every move to what Jóska would have done in a similar situation. Physically, Steven was shorter, and he had a receding hairline; his blue eyes were a bit too close together. Steven lacked the easy charm with which Jóska controlled people and situations. I had no illusions about my reasons for marrying him, and neither did he.

Everyone needed a guide as minefields had been laid along the border and guards with attack dogs patrolled. The border being "open" simply meant that someone had figured out a way to penetrate the minefields and had obtained a schedule of the patrols.

"The poppies are starting to bloom near Szombathely," said the voice on the telephone one morning in April. Steven had arranged for this coded message to trigger our second attempt to escape across the border.

"Great, we'll be there tomorrow," I replied.

The next morning, we took the train just as we had before. When we reached Szombathely in the afternoon, the guide, who went by the code name of Miklós, seemed optimistic. We met him, per his telephone instructions, behind a dairy on the outskirts of town.

"Meet me at *Cigany Janci*'s at nine sharp," Miklós then told us, giving us directions to a small tavern on a side street. "Don't be late." He promised to take us across by car.

At the tavern we ordered venison to use up our Hungarian cash which would be useless across the border. It happened to be the most expensive dish on the menu. A gypsy played his violin while we ate, his tunes evoking memories of my sixteenth birthday at Szekszárd. I felt my eyes mist.

"Are you all right, Éva?" Steven asked.

"The music is getting to me," I replied, not wanting to elaborate. Most of the time it felt as though I had a stone where my heart should be, but gypsy music evoked emotions I did not want to feel ever again. Steven had to have been just as aware as I that in a short while we would be leaving Hungary, probably forever. *To leave one's country is to die a little,* I thought.

The clock on the wall inched toward nine. Miklós, our guide, entered the tavern through the rear door and beckoned to us to follow him. We paid our bill and exited the tavern by a side door, which opened onto an unlit alley.

Miklós led us to a dark sedan parked at the curb. He motioned for us to join a young couple huddled in the back seat. I climbed in next to them, while Steven sat in front with the guide.

"I'm Anna," the woman introduced herself. "We have three children. It seems too cruel. Do you think we'll get across?" She murmured and rambled, emitting a nervous laugh from time to time. She appeared to be terrified.

As I listened to Anna's recitation, a strange calmness descended on me. Everything imaginable had already happened to me, and I did not really care what came next.

When Oberlieutenant Weiss commanded me to lick his boot, it was as if he had poured concrete around my heart, which had then hardened completely when Jóska took his own life. Had it not been for some deep primordial instinct to keep myself alive for the sake of the children, I would have gladly followed Jóska to the grave. Instead, my life now was linked to Steven's, for whom I had no deep feelings.

The guide rolled the car down the slight incline, leading away from the tavern, without turning on the engine or the headlights. After coasting the length of a block away from the center of town, he cranked the motor but drove without lights. Cold air whistled through a crack in the car window. We turned onto a gravel road, the wheels crunching the stones so loudly I felt the whole world could hear. The woman huddled next to me sobbed. I shivered in spite of my close proximity to her in the back seat.

After fifteen minutes of driving west toward the border, away from Szombathely, a searchlight illuminated the car.

"Out—quick," ordered Miklós.

We scrambled to exit the car. My coat caught in the door. I couldn't get it loose. I tugged at it clumsily while hanging on to my suitcase with my other hand. My mind just wouldn't function; I couldn't think what to do.

"Take it off," Steven commanded. I slipped my arms out of the coat and dashed after the others, heading into a plowed field.

So, I thought, expecting a mine to blow us up any second, *we will at least go with a bang, not a whimper.* Pitch dark again as the searchlight moved on. Perhaps no one was manning it.

We crawled, feeling our way through the moonless night, dragging our belongings. Steven led, and I followed as best I could. Rocks and hardened clumps of earth cut at my hands and knees. The field seemed endless. I felt very much afraid. *Where are you, Jóska, when I need you so?*

The searchlight swept past once again, illuminating our progress as well as the edge of some woods on the far side of the field. The five of us tried to flatten ourselves into the earth and held our breath. Then darkness descended once again. I heard a whimper coming from Anna, who was crawling behind me.

"Shut up and move on," came the whispered order from our guide, who brought up the rear.

"Faster, faster," he said as the woman kept sniffling.

Then, just as we reached the edge of the woods, out of range of the spotlight, dogs began barking. My heart raced along with my mind.

"My God," Miklós exclaimed. "The sons of bitches set the dogs on us."

Following his lead, Steven and I leaped to our feet and ran, stumbling through the underbrush, branches slapping our faces and tearing our clothes. With iron calm, Steven quietly urged us on. The dogs were coming closer, and, in our panicky state, they seemed to be all around us. The barking became a staccato, punctuating the pounding of our hearts and feet and the crackling of leaves underfoot. Just as I thought my lungs would burst and my arms drop off from lugging my suitcase, we broke through the far side of the woods. A pale moon shone through the clouds, and we could see the outlines of a house about one hundred yards ahead.

"It must be Austria," hissed the guide from behind us. "Run for it."

I felt a surge of hope, and then I crashed into the back of Steven, who had stopped in his tracks. At the same instant, I was leaped upon by a massive shape from behind and bowled over.

This is it, I thought, expecting the dog's teeth to sink into my jugular at any moment.

I heard Steven command, "Down, boy!" just as I felt a sloppy tongue lick my face.

These weren't guard dogs, but three exuberant St. Bernard

puppies out for a late-night romp. I disentangled myself from the bouncing, licking bundle of fur and scrambled to my feet. I had a vision of puppies playing at Cservölgy. Weariness and relief overcame me.

Lights went on, the door of the farmhouse opened, and we heard "Hansel, Spatzle, Gretl, *kommt hier!*"

"Austria," whooped the guide behind us as we all stumbled toward the house.

We had made it across.

In the morning, the farmer drove us in a horse-drawn cart to a depot in a neighboring village. He told us that the bus always traveled without incident to Vienna from there; it had never been stopped. The farmer said that this was not his first encounter with refugees. We were still in the Russian zone, however, which encircled Vienna at the time. Vienna itself was divided into four zones, just like Berlin: American, English, French, and Russian.

The bus pulled up in a few minutes, and we climbed aboard. Seated near the exit were several Russian soldiers, smoking, drinking, talking, and laughing. They paid no attention to us. I sat down in a single seat right behind Steven.

In the middle of the Vienerwald, the forest near Vienna, the bus halted. A young Austrian soldier boarded.

"Passports, please," he demanded. I was horrified: we had made it this far, and now we would be arrested, doubtless transported back to Hungary, and imprisoned.

The soldier walked down the aisle toward us, inspecting documents. The Russians paid no attention.

"Passport, please," the young Austrian said, holding out his hand to Steven.

"I am a Hungarian army officer, trying to escape. That's my wife sitting behind me. We have no papers." Steven spoke in a low voice in German, handing the soldier the menu he had pocketed at the Hungarian restaurant near the border, pretending it constituted a travel document.

I thought it was only in novels that time stood still. But it certainly stopped for a minute right then.

There was an almost imperceptible click of the soldier's heels.

"Thank you, sir," he said, as he handed back the menu and moved on.

Steven had assessed the situation, saw the one and only chance we had, which was to tell the truth, and he had taken it.

Only later did I realize that in my coat pocket, left hanging in the car door at the minefield, was not only the marriage certificate but the cyanide. Would I have used it if we had been arrested? I'll never know.

We arrived in the American sector of a dreary, bombed-out Vienna, and went to a safe house at an address our guide had given us. A very unpleasant couple let us spend the night on their floor but offered us no food. In the morning, we went straight to the Office of Strategic Services, the forerunner of the Central Intelligence Agency.

Alerted by Walt Maher, the vice counsel who had traveled to Cservölgy in the red school bus, the OSS officials treated us well. They had Steven draw them a map of our escape route and then sent us to a house where we were given a good meal and a decent bed.

"Can you pay?" our host asked. "If not, it's free."

He also gave me a warm gray coat for which I was most grateful, to replace the one I had lost in the border crossing.

The OSS provided us with false passports for our crossing of the Enns Bridge out of Vienna, and the next day Steven and I arrived in Salzburg without further incident. We had escaped. Where there should have been a feeling of elation, I felt only an infinite weariness.

A few days later, I found a job with the U.S. War Crimes Court then in session, but Steven could find no employment. Because of that, after a few weeks, we obtained permits to move to Innsbruck, where the International Refugee Organization needed Hungarian French-speaking workers to process the flow of people arriving from the east. International organizations used French as their common language, so the processing of refugees generally transpired in that language. Both Steven and I spoke French and were hired.

We hoped to send for the girls to come from Switzerland, as soon as we could find adequate housing, and support them.

We started the process of applying for immigration to a number of Western countries.

The Survivors

The commissioners of the International Refugee
Organization (IRO), our employers, came from various countries.
Little tin gods, all of them. Few of them had ever had such important
jobs before. They ate at the best restaurants and often decided hungry
refugees' fates while under the influence of alcohol.

One day, I was confronted by a waiting room full of
Hungarians who wanted to go to Chile. The Chilean commissioner
patted my shoulder. "What you say goes," he said.

I went out of my office and quietly told the Hungarians that
I could probably get all twenty-four of them onto the next ship. I
asked them to pretend they did not speak a word of French, whether
they knew the language or not, and to let me communicate with the
Chilean official in charge. The Chilean big shot kept his word and
accepted them all. The refugees were elated. Many of them kissed
my hand.

Any destination in the Americas was regarded as heaven in those
days. I was pleased that I had been able to help my countrymen. They
sailed from Cherbourg, France, in what was reported to be an old
cargo vessel, not much bigger than a bathtub.

A week or two later, the Chilean official announced that the
ship carrying the Hungarians had sunk, somewhere in the Atlantic.
There were no survivors. I felt devastated that I had sent the twenty-
four Hungarians to their deaths.

I shuddered at the thought that if Livia and Ági had already
arrived in Innsbruck from Switzerland, Steven and I, as well as the
children, could well have been on that boat.

A Polish farm family came repeatedly to the International
Refugee Organization office, even though their case seemed
hopeless. None of the countries accepting immigrants wanted
farmers. The family was further hampered by the young man's father

who had escaped with the family. He was in his seventies. No one wanted old people.

"I'm sorry, I told you not to come today," I said to Palcsi, the young husband, when they walked in one day for what seemed like the hundredth time.

Palcsi put the family's documents on the table as usual. The head of the Brazilian commission, who was passing by my desk, thumbed through them. He picked up a yellow parchment. He turned to the old man. "Are you a watchmaker by profession?"

"Yes, sir. I have been a watchmaker in our village for fifty years," Palcsi's father replied with evident pride.

"Accepted," said the Brazilian commissioner. "I suppose we can let the family go along as dependents," he added.

Roles reversed, the old man motioned his family to follow. He walked into the next room with godlike dignity, his son and grandchildren trailing after him.

Another commissioner, glancing at the family portrait attached to an application, crossed off the picture of a very old woman who was standing in line along with her son and his family. "She can't go. The rest of you are accepted."

The old woman keeled over in a faint.

"No thanks. I am not leaving without her," her son said as he bent down to help his mother.

"Suit yourself," shrugged the tin god, sending the refugees back to languish in a camp.

Word spread that the Canadians wanted miners. People became miners overnight. Baggy work clothes replaced threadbare suits, applications were rewritten and degrees dropped.

Medical inspectors pried the applicants' mouths open to see whether they had healthy teeth, further stripping the refugees of dignity. The Canadians wanted the men to be over a certain weight. Steven heard of that requirement and put stones in the would-be-miners' pockets.

To our joy, twenty families immigrated to Canadian mining towns.

Working for the IRO was a daily reminder to Steven and me of the horrors we had experienced and the fates we had managed to escape.

As refugees poured in, we learned a lot of things. It became clear to us that in the end, many Jews in Budapest had been spared the ultimate horror. We heard of a rich Swedish diplomat, Raoul Wallenberg, who had used his own wealth to bribe the German High Command to stall the transports. On the other hand, nearly all the inmates of camps in the countryside had perished.

One refugee told us that hundreds of Jews from the region near Szekszárd and Cservölgy had been herded into cattle cars and taken to a ghetto in Dombovár. In June 1944, the inhabitants of that camp were transferred to Birkenau in Poland and exterminated.

A young blond Hungarian woman named Edith came to the office one day and applied for immigration to America. She recognized my name, and said she knew my parents, and knew my cousin Ágota, after whom my Ági had been named. I did not recall ever having met Edith. She wore a sleeveless white dress that revealed an ugly welt, the size of a quarter, on her upper arm.

"What's that?" I asked. "Did you hurt yourself?"

"Haven't you seen that before? It's an Auschwitz mark." She had been branded like an animal. "My parents and my brother were gassed." She smiled an enigmatic smile.

"You know, I was on the same transport as Ágota's fourteen-month-old son," she sighed. "I told your cousin that the child was gassed, but it wasn't true.

"You see, there were three young boys, little Sándor and two twelve-year-olds. The Nazis saw right away that the older boys were very weak and that it wouldn't be any use to try to force them to work. They threw them to some bloodhounds they kept in a pit. They held little Sándor until last. He was screaming. The guard who held him flung him by one leg into the pit." Her voice trailed off, but her face reflected the horror of her memories.

Another day, a ghost from the past appeared. Iluci's in-laws had been in the ghetto house with my parents in Budapest. I used to see Iluci playing with her children in the hallway when I went to take food to my parents. She and her husband Miska had both been deported and had left their two little sons with her in-laws at the ghetto house.

"The day we reported to the train station as ordered," Iluci related, "Miska was helping me carry my suitcase; we'd been told to bring only one each. There were hundreds of people inside the depot, milling about, quietly talking, apprehension etched on their faces. We had all been told to leave our children behind with relatives. Suddenly the order came over the loudspeakers: 'Women stand to the left, men to the right please. NOW!' It hadn't occurred to us that we would be separated. I panicked.

"'Perhaps it's just for a count,' Miska had said, sensing my anxiety. He had moved his hand over mine on the suitcase handle as he walked to the left with me. Then his path was blocked by a German soldier, who sneered at him and yelled, 'TO THE RIGHT, SIR!'

"Miska, giving my hand a squeeze, handed something to me and moved away to the other side of the depot. I looked down and realized that my husband had given me one of our baby's diaper pins. For months now he had been wearing one, stuck through his yellow Star of David, as an affirmation that he was born a Jew and 'proud of it,' he had said.

"Tears filled my eyes as I took the pin and stuck it through my own star. *A part of Miska is still with me,* I thought. At that moment my husband looked back at me, smiled, and pointed at his own chest. The station lights glinted off his matching pin and then he was gone. I never saw him again.

"In the midst of the steam released from a nearby engine, they marched us off toward a check-in station where we were told to approach one at a time. The three officers seated at a table conferred briefly after they looked each person over, and then pointed to one or the other of two waiting passenger trains. My turn came. I felt like a piece of meat hanging in a butcher shop, when they looked me up and down, peeling me naked with their eyes. No words were spoken. One of them just pointed with a glimmer of amusement in his eyes. I climbed aboard the train, feeling the officers' eyes on my legs." Iluci closed her eyes for a moment.

"It must have been awful for you," I said to give her time to compose herself.

"I looked around," she continued, "and found my companions to be young, good- looking, able-bodied women. I shuddered, since I'd heard of brothel trains provided for the German troops.

"We started out with great apprehension, but we were not ill-treated. Since we were on a passenger train, there were toilet facilities and tiny sinks in each car. Each of us had a double upholstered seat to sleep on, and they fed us regularly. The train was shuttled back and forth for weeks. We never knew where we were or where we were going. Signs at train depots had been obliterated, perhaps to hinder advancing enemy troops. We kept guessing about what would happen next. Most nights we spent at a siding in the middle of open fields, never near a town. The tension, each time we came to a stop, became unbearable. Every time a group of soldiers approached the train, we thought: *This is it—now we will be raped.* But each time, nothing happened. The guards would give us no information.

"'We have our orders,' was all our guards would say.

"We had no idea what had become of our husbands, how the war was going, what was happening to our children, nothing. Sometimes our train stood on a siding for days. Tension and bickering over trivia mounted among the women. We had no clue what would become of us. I rubbed my diaper pin and held my tongue to avoid getting embroiled in arguments," Edith noted.

"We had an unwritten rule never to look at pictures of our children. It was our way of disassociating ourselves from everything except the task of keeping alive. We played word games, told each other stories, taught each other languages, trying to stay mentally alert. I caught myself fingering that diaper pin, stroking it for hours. It was my link to Miska and the children and my defiance of my captors.

"Then one day the train pulled into a station. We guessed we might be somewhere in Poland. A group of young women was added to the transport. They had been deported with their children. Éva, I don't know how to describe it, but when one of those children sat down next to me, something inside me gave way. I could not stop sobbing and shaking. All up and down the train the same thing was happening. Women who had endured months of uncertainty with stoicism were suddenly driven to some kind of frenzy by the sight of those children. Mothers started crying and talking incoherently.

"Those became the most spoiled children in the world. When the new arrivals realized that we had all been separated from our children, they shared theirs with us and there were lots of hugging and outpourings of pent-up love on those little ones. We told the boys and girls stories in Hungarian, even though they were Polish. They didn't seem to mind.

"The weeks stretched into our third month as we were shuttled from siding to siding, depot to depot. Never-ending nights."

Edith paused with a faraway look in her eyes.

"Believe it or not, Éva, it was the strangest thing. Absolutely nothing happened to us.

"One morning, we woke at a remote siding. The sun was higher in the sky than on previous days, and we realized that our guards had not awakened us. Something was wrong. The usual sounds of breakfast preparations were missing. We only heard the noises on the train of people waking, children stirring. I looked out the window and saw no field kitchen, no one, and nothing in sight. I walked through several of the train cars. No guards. I tried to open one of the doors leading to the platform and found it unlocked. It dawned on me that we had been abandoned by our captors.

"I walked through the length of the train shouting: 'The Nazis are gone, we are free! THE WAR MUST BE OVER!!!'

"'What shall we do? Where do we go? Where are we?' came the unanswerable questions.

"Women and children rushed off the train, dragging their meager possessions and talking excitedly. They tried to find identifying marks in the surrounding area. We didn't even know what country we were in, and there seemed nothing in sight but fields and woods. A road parallel to the siding seemed to be our only connection to civilization. The women discussed what to do. We decided that some of us should walk in one direction, while others went in the opposite one. There were promises of returning for those with young children, once we knew where we were.

"Just as we set off, a jeep drove into view. Our hearts sank. Our captors were back, and we had wasted precious time and didn't get away. But no, as the jeep drew closer, we saw a tattered British flag attached to its front bumper. We were liberated!

"After the jubilation subsided, the Brits informed us we were in Germany, and arranged to have the train taken back to Budapest. The German women among us were transported by bus to their hometowns.

"I tore my Star of David off my chest, being careful to disengage the diaper pin which had become my talisman. When, days later, we reached Budapest, I started out on foot for our house, walking through destroyed neighborhoods, one hand dragging my suitcase, the other rubbing hard on that pin. I left the suitcase by our front door but just couldn't go in. I walked around the block three times, rubbing away at that pin, talking to myself, vacillating between hope and despair: 'They must be all right. They just have to be.' 'There won't be anybody there.'

"At last, I gathered my courage and rang the bell. My mother-in-law peered out, then threw open the door. The little ones, unharmed, stood hiding behind her, playing peek-a-boo. They had no concept of the eternity that had passed since we last saw each other several months ago.

"'Miska died in a German army barracks,' my mother-in-law said in response to the unasked question in my eyes. 'A fellow prisoner who survived came to see us a week ago,' she added. I opened my arms and the children came running into them, overwhelming me with bittersweet emotions."

To The Promised Land

The stability of Steven's and my job with the International Refugee Organization seemed assured by the unending stream of refugees coming over the borders from Eastern Europe. We decided to send for Livia and Ági to come from Switzerland to join us. They were thirteen and eleven by this time.

A year had passed since I had seen my daughters. Though overjoyed at their arrival, I was shocked to see them step off the train, Ági clutching her gold bear, and both children looking considerably thinner than when they had left Hungary. Livia had fared somewhat better than Ági, as she had been able to babysit the two young children of the family with whom she had stayed.

"We'd get up at four in the morning to milk the cows," Ági related, "and finish the day knitting socks for the men in the family. Boy, I was tired by bedtime at ten."

Both host families were strict Calvinists, stern and rigid. Ági related that *Mutti*, the mother of the Swiss household where she had stayed, considered dancing and music to be sinful and had told her that I would roast in hell when Ági mentioned that I played the piano.

"We didn't have to go to school," Livia informed us, "because we had too much work to do. *Fatti*, the head of the household, believed school to be a waste of time."

"I never wrote you about the bugs, did I?" Ági asked me that evening, and told of a locust infestation during which she had helped gather the bugs by hand off the trees to keep them from devouring the blossoming fruit buds. Insecticides seemed to be unavailable.

"We couldn't see the sun. There were black clouds of them," she related.

I should have listened to my parents and kept the children home in Hungary, I thought as I listened to her. What had I been trying to do anyway?

As our stay in Austria lengthened into its fourth month, Steven grumbled that he wanted to return to Hungary.

"We must be realistic," I told him during one conversation on the subject. "There is no turning back. We have no home now." I realized as I spoke these words that we had to create some sort of permanence in our situation soon, either by emigrating or applying for permanent residence in Austria, so that we could get on with our new lives.

In February 1949, Argentina granted Steven, me, and the children visas. We had two weeks to decide whether to accept, or hinge our hopes on the possibility that at some time in the future we might be admitted to the United States.

"Steven, we should go to Argentina with the Szabos." The Szabos, fellow Hungarians, lived in one of the refugee camps and we had become friends. "At least we'll know someone there."

"The place is crawling with Nazis! I want nothing to do with Argentina," Steven replied with unaccustomed vehemence.

The next day, however, he came home from work and announced, "I have accepted the Argentinean visa and signed us all up for Spanish classes. We leave on April first."

To my relief, Steven had made the decision for all of us. In the next few weeks, he and I read everything we could lay our hands on about Argentina, since neither of us knew much about the country or its people.

In March 1949, just as we had resigned ourselves to the idea of spending the rest of our lives in Argentina, an envelope stamped "Official Business" from the Department of State of the United States of America arrived at the residential hotel where we had been living. I took it out of our mailbox as though the envelope were a land mine and carried it to our room and placed it on the dressing table. I couldn't bring myself to open it. Then I picked it up again and held it in front of the window. The only word I could make out through the airmail tissue was "regret."

So, even though Steven had risked his life during the war feeding information to the Americans from the Ukraine, they don't want us after all, I thought.

I dumped the envelope back on the dresser without opening it. I hoped that when Steven read it, he wouldn't be too upset. *Buenos Aires can't be that bad,* I thought. A sizeable Hungarian community already existed there.

Steven came home and spotted the envelope. "Why haven't you read it?" he asked, grabbing it and ripping it open.

"What does it say?"

"Éva—we are in!" he exclaimed as he started reading.

"'Dear Colonel Molnár,' it says, 'you and your wife have been accepted for immigration to the United States and will be given permanent refugee status.'"

Thrilling news! AMERICA!

"'We regret to inform you,'" Steven read on, "'that your daughters must wait until they have been in Austria for six months before their cases can be given consideration.'"

A Catch-22 situation! If we refused the visa, our names would go to the bottom of the list. The girls in turn would be offered admittance when their six months' wait was up. Then they would have permission to enter the United States, but Steven and I would not.

If we accepted the visa being offered to us, we'd have to leave Livia and Ági behind, and pray that nothing happened to stem the flow of entry permits into the United States between the time that we left and when their names reached the top of the list. Listening to the Voice of America, an international news service broadcast by the United States, we had heard of grumbling in the American press about the number of immigrants to be absorbed, and speeches made in the U.S. Senate about trimming the quotas.

"Leaving the girls behind is out of the question," Steven said, relieving me of having to make the decision.

Just at that moment Livia and Ági burst in, home from school. They could see from our faces that something important had happened before we even told them the news. Livia seemed relieved that there would not be another separation.

"You are throwing away the Nobel Prize of visas? Why can't we stay at school, while you two go on ahead?" Ági chimed in on the conversation. The girls attended the day program at a boarding school in Innsbruck.

I tried to think of an answer. Steven picked up the phone and called the American consulate. We all listened intently to hear what he would say. He rejected the visa and told the official why. Then he listened for quite some time without saying a word.

"I'll get back to you," he said, hanging up the phone.

The vice-consul had suggested that Steven and I go to America, and from there try to move heaven and earth to expedite the entry of the two girls on humanitarian grounds.

"There have been such cases with good results," the American told Steven.

We stayed up half the night, weighing the pros and cons, and decided that we couldn't pass up the chance to go to America after all. The children's future hinged on our decision. If worst came to worst, and the girls were denied entry within a reasonable time, we could return to Austria, although where we'd get the money for such a trip, we had no idea.

Both girls were very excited at the prospect of seeing the United States. With the last of our money, we checked the girls into a boarding school run by the Ursuline nuns and appeased Livia by telling her the separation would be a short one. Ági started concocting plans for adventures while on their own.

We telegraphed my cousin Peter, who had reached New York

in 1946, and had agreed to be our official sponsor. Among the refugees, everyone seemed to have a cousin in New York, and we were no exception.

We made airline reservations, and sold the gold coins Ági had carried to Switzerland inside her bear to pay the fare. Then the authorities informed us that due to some new quirk in the regulations, we must go by ship rather than by air. We bribed the travel agent to get our airfare back. The regulations said we had to go by train to Cherbourg, France, and thence by ship to New York.

Our friends, the Szabos, lacked any American connections and had no realistic hope for an American visa. They continued with their plans to go to Argentina in a few weeks. When the morning for our departure arrived, they came to the train station with us, so the girls could see us off. After much hugging and kissing all around and promises of good behavior on the part of the children, Steven and I climbed aboard the train.

I looked out the window. Livia and Ági stood on the platform with the Szabos, who would soon depart for their new life in Buenos Aires. They had been good friends to us. I felt sad that I would never see them again.

As for Livia and Ági, they didn't appear to be depressed. They stood there, fidgeting in their uniforms, anxious to get to school and see their friends. They seemed to have adapted to this latest development in their circumstances. My last sight of them was of sunlight glinting off two auburn heads as they ran on the platform trying to keep up with the departing train. My heart sank as their faces were obliterated by distance.

I leaned back on the seat with Steven sitting opposite. He looked as tired as I felt. The train wound its way through the Austrian Alps, minute by minute putting more distance between the children and me. I was bone weary from the tensions of the past months and the preparations for our departure. Though Steven talked to me of plans he had for the time when we reached New York, I ceased to listen.

A man wearing a skullcap walked past our compartment. I had not seen one of those since long before the war. I tried to make sense of the mixed emotions the sight of that yarmulke evoked in me. My mind wandered over the twisted road that had brought me to this point, from the time when I had been a child and my grandpa would visit, wearing a yarmulke. I loved him and had felt uneasy when people made fun of him. Then Grandpa died. Looking back over the years, I could understand that I had been surrounded by the trappings of Catholicism and had lost all connection to my Jewish ancestors. I remembered mocking Jewish children while in grammar school and that I had felt no affinity to them whatsoever.

My thoughts from the early days of the war came back to me, when I felt that Hitler's anti-Semitism had nothing to do with me. I mused about having been fawned over at the French tea and then having realized that I was not wanted there. I relived in my mind the hatred and humiliation I had felt when the full horror of the Nazis descended on me in the shape of a boot. Yet, I thought, I resented the Jews who had watched my humiliation and done nothing to help me. Jóska had been ambivalent about Jews. Yet he had loved me as I had loved him. How could I make sense of any of this? Though a Catholic, I was never devout. I had no answer to why we were put on this earth, except to do our best to make a few people happy around us. The rest perhaps didn't matter.

The train stopped at a mountain village, and the pause interrupted my reverie. Steven opened the window of our compartment, and music drifted in from the café at the station. I closed my eyes to avoid conversation and continued to ruminate. In my mind's eye I was back in our prewar apartment in Budapest, seated at the piano with my two little daughters crowded on the bench beside me: Jóska stood in the doorway, watching us.

"Sing 'She'll Be Coming Round the Mountain,'" the girls intoned. For the hundredth time I sang them the tune they loved best, even though they didn't understand most of the words.

"She'll be coming round the mountain when she comes. She'll be driving six white horses, she'll be driving six white horses, she'll be driving six white horses when she comes."

Somehow, sitting on that train, that song embodied my longing for my children and Jóska.

The rhythmic clanging of the wheels along the tracks was interrupted by a long, haunting whistle as we plunged into a dark tunnel.

I woke with a start: Steven was leaning toward me, talking to me. In a state between dreaming and waking, "She'll be coming round the mountain..." floated through my consciousness. I felt a longing for Jóska to come and take care of me.

The train emerged from the tunnel, and I glimpsed the tracks gleaming in the afternoon sun, stretching ahead and leading us toward our unknown future.

Epilogue by Agatha Hoff

After their arrival in America, toward the end of March 1949, my mother Éva and stepfather Steven bombarded the authorities with requests to expedite Livia's and my immigration. Six anxious months passed before my sister and I were allowed entry into the United States in September.

Our reunited family moved to San Francisco, where we followed the immigrant ethic, forging new lives through hard work and education.

Mama had just turned fifty-one, when, in October 1956, a revolt broke out in Hungary against the Communist government and the continuing Russian occupation. Éva, my mother, was offered a job as an editorial writer for the Voice of America in Washington, D.C. For the rest of her life, she would regret writing broadcasts encouraging the freedom fighters who had been full of hope and expectation. Lack of help from the West doomed the uprising, and many Hungarians died. In the radio studio, my mother listened to desperate pleas on Hungarian radio and heard gunfire mowing down the broadcasters in Budapest, as the radio station was retaken by Russian troops.

After that, Mama suffered repeated nightmares, seeing bodies floating in the Danube, burning horses, and bayonets, as her memories of World War II mixed in her subconscious with the horrors of the failed revolt.

Remembrances of her years with my father Jóska continued to dominate her life.

Mama's grandson—one of my sons, named Joe after Papa—bears a remarkable resemblance to Jóska. The similarity created a special bond between my mother and my son. To link their family to our history, Joe and his wife Laurie named one of their twin daughters Eva, after my mother.

Having left Hungary illegally, it was not until Livia and I both were married and after Steven died that, in 1972, Mama risked returning to Hungary for the first of many visits. She relished the atmosphere in Budapest and encountered family, friends, and memories at every turn.

As the years passed, my mother's eyesight deteriorated and her mind began to fail. She applied for admission to the Jewish Home for the Aged when she reached age eighty-five. During the war, Mama had destroyed all documents connecting her to her Jewish ancestry. She had to obtain affidavits attesting to her lineage to present with her application. Although she had been Jewish enough for Hitler, she wasn't Jewish enough for the Jewish Home. Her application for admission was rejected because she had never become affiliated with a temple and had raised my sister Livia and me as Catholics.

Though residing with Livia, Mama lived more and more in the past and made references to wanting to go home to Jóska. On January 17, 1992, at age eighty-six, she overdosed on sleeping pills and died while listening to Beethoven's Fifth Symphony on her ancient record player.

"I love you all very much. Don't be sad. I have loved and been loved and I am ready to go. I am going home to Papa," she wrote in a note she left on her bedside table. Referring to her namesake, she continued, "Little Eva, carry on." Mama had retained her sense of humor to the end and penned a postscript to her suicide note, "Have them say a Mass for me, it can't hurt..."

Then came the last ironic twist of Mama's turbulent life. She had told us that after she died, her ashes should be interred in Budapest with Papa. The Catholic cemetery refused permission for the burial, however, because Mama was a Jew. Livia had to fax them the fake birth certificate our mother had acquired during World War II. It showed Éva's family to be Catholic four generations back.

Finally, the powers that be allowed the funeral to take place.

My mother had often told Livia and me not to waste money on traveling to her funeral. Obeying her wishes, neither of us went to Hungary for the ceremony. On the day of Mama's burial, however, she couldn't stop my thoughts from wandering the hillsides of my childhood. That night, I dreamed I was at Cservölgy. Climbing the stairs to our former nursery, I heard again Livia's young voice in a sleepy cadence, counting clouds rolling by, then my grandma's voice calling us from the veranda: "LIIIVIA, ÁGOTA, TIME TO COME HOME…"

In my dream, I ran downstairs looking for Grandma, but the house was empty and the veranda outside the living room crumbling. An unknown person had spray-painted graffiti on the dining room wall: "What kind of people are we that we allow a beautiful house like this to fall into ruin?"

I noticed Papa's old shortwave radio in a cobwebbed corner and heard again the booming voice of Winston Churchill:

"We shall never surrender."

I could hear Mama's voice translating the English into Hungarian and somehow knew Churchill's words had been the unspoken motto of my mother's life. Somewhere between waking and sleeping, I became aware that I would have to leave the house and return to the present, but I didn't want the dream to end before going outside to see the woods once more. Willing myself to focus on the dream, I walked out the big front door and noted the weeds beginning to grow over the threshold and waiting to cover a life that once thrived in that house. I began to cry.

I pulled the door shut behind me and, through my tears, looked toward the nearby forest. It was dusk, and nothing disturbed the rustling of the leaves. As I looked at those well-remembered woods, I saw a figure emerging from among the trees. For a moment, I thought it was Papa and ran toward him. Then the man turned to face me, and what a moment ago had appeared to be my father became my son Joe. Trailing from the woods behind him came his two little girls, Sarah and Eva, just as Livia and I had trailed behind Papa long, long ago.

Hungarian Jewish Timeline

"There is no doubt that this persecution of Jews in Hungary and their expulsion from enemy territory is probably the greatest and most horrible crime ever committed in the whole history of the world..."

Winston Churchill
11 July 1944

Pre-World War I

1867-1914

- Hungary is part of the Austro-Hungarian Empire
- Austrian Emperor Franz Josef I is King of Hungary

World War I

1914-1918

World War I conflict between the Triple Alliance (Germany, Austria-Hungary, and Italy) and Triple Entente (Britain, France, and Russia) set in motion with the assassination of Archduke Francis Ferdinand, heir to the Austrian throne, in Sarajevo on 28 June 1914.

1918

- World War I ends
- Hungarian monarchy, allied with Germany, is defeated
- First post-war government is a liberal democratic government led by Mihály Károlyi

March, 1919

- Coalition government of Communists and Social Democrats ousts Károlyi and his party
- Communists, led by Béla Kun and several other Jewish leaders,

take control of the government and form the Hungarian
Soviet Republic

<u>July, 1919</u>
- After 133 days, Béla Kun's regime is defeated and replaced by
the government of former Austro-Hungarian admiral and
anti-Semite, Miklós Horthy
- Horthy's National Army initiates the White Terror, a series of
pogroms directed at Jews, progressives, peasants and others

<u>1920</u>
- Horthy's government passes a number of anti-Jewish laws,
including a "Numerus Clausus," restricting Jewish enrollment
at universities to 5%, based on their percentage of the
Hungarian population

<u>1938-1941</u>
- Anti-Jewish laws become more repressive
- 29 May 1938 — First Jewish Law
The number of Jews in business, the press, medicine, law and
engineering is restricted to 20%
- 5 May 1939 — Second Jewish Law
Jews are defined racially, not by religion. Individuals with
two, three or four Jewish-born grandparents are considered
Jewish.
Jews are:
  - Forbidden to work in the government
  - Forbidden to work as newspaper editors
  - Restricted to 5% of physicians, lawyers, engineers and
  theatre and movie actors
  - Restricted to be 12% of the employee population of any
  private company

- 8 August 1941 – Third Jewish Law
  - Intermarriage between Jews and gentiles is forbidden
  - Extramarital sexual relations between a Jewish man and a gentile woman are punishable by three years' imprisonment
- July-August 1941
  - Hungary deports 20,000 Jews to Kamenets-Podolsk, Ukraine, where they are murdered

1942
- Hungary's anti-Semitic prime minister, Miklos Kallay orders that all Jewish property be expropriated

1944
- 19 March - Nazis invade Hungary
- April
  - 400,000 Jews are removed from Hungarian towns, cities and villages to ghettos
  - Jews are ordered to wear yellow Star of David
  - Jewish businesses are closed
  - Jews are forbidden to ride public transportation or visit public places
- 15 May – Deportation of Hungarian Jews to Auschwitz begins
- 15 October – The fascist, anti-Semitic Arrow Cross Party deposes Horthy and takes over the Hungarian government
- November 1944 – February 1945 – The Arrow Cross Party shoots 15,000 Jews on the banks of the Danube River
- 27 December – Soviet troops begin the Battle of Budapest

1945
- 18 January - Soviet Army captures Budapest and liberates the Budapest ghetto
- 26 January – Soviet Army liberates Auschwitz
- 4 April – War in Hungary ends

References

Crowe, David M. The Holocaust: Roots, History, and Aftermath. Boulder, Colorado: Westview Press, 2008. Book excerpts online at books.google.com/books?isbn=0813343259.

Patai, Raphael. The Jews of Hungary: History, Culture, Psychology. Detroit: Wayne State University Press, 1996. Book excerpts online at books.google.com/books?isbn=0814325610

The Virtual Jewish History Tour-Hungary, www.jewishvirtuallibrary.org/jsource/vjw/Hungary.html

Simon, Istvan. "Winston Churchill's The Second World War and the Holocaust's Uniqueness," http://cgi.stanford.edu/group/wais/cgi-bin/index.php?p=6855

Other Pertinent Books on the Jewish Holocaust

Denes, Magda. *Castles Burning: A Child's Life in War,* New York: W.W.
Norton & Co., 1997, ISBN: 9780393039665.
A child's perspective of the horrors of war. Hungarian Jew
Magda Denes'childhood was interrupted in 1939 when her father
abandoned his young family and fled to New York City. Magda and
the relatives with whom she lived from 1939 to 1946 faced poverty
and starvation as they hid from the soldiers of fascist Hungary and as
displaced persons in post-World War II Germany.

Gilles, Elisabeth (Linda Coverdale, Translator). *Shadows of a Childhood:
A Novel of War and Friendship,* New York: New Press, 1998,
ISBN: 9781565843882.
A fictionalized, first-person account of the thirteen years of Lea
Levy's World War II childhood experiences, including the separation
from her mother who was deported to a concentration camp, never
to be seen again. The book details Lea's healing friendship with her
Catholic adopted sister with whom she explores and ponders the
tragic world in which they live.

Grimbert, Philippe. *Memory: A Novel,* New York, Simon & Schuster,
2008, ISBN: 9781416559993.
Melding memoir and fiction, French psychoanalyst Grimbert revisits
the secrets that dominated his parents' life during World War II in
occupied France. This fictionalized account was written twenty years
after his parents jumped to their deaths.

Grove, Andrew. *Swimming Across: A Memoir,* New York: Warner Books,
2001, ISBN: 9780446528595 (paperback).
Swimming Across is the autobiography of Andras Grof in pre-World
War II Hungary, during the Hungarian Holocaust when his father

was sent to a labor camp, through the harsh living conditions of the 1956 revolution, and his new beginning in America. In his new country he changed his name to Andrew Grove, eventually became co-founder and chairman of Intel (a high tech research and manufacturing corporation), and earned the title of *Time*'s 1997 Man of the Year.

Hauptman, Sara. *The Lioness of Judah: A Lion Tamer's Memoir of Resistance and Survival*, Colorado Springs: Dancing Queens Press, 2006, ISBN: 0009785123089 (paperback).
This is the story of a Belgian, Jewish woman who used her job as a lion tamer to serve as a cover for her resistance activities. It recounts her eventual arrest and her experiences as a victim of concentration camp medical experiments.

Lourie, Richard. *Joop: A Novel of Anne Frank*, New York: Thomas Dunne Books, 2008, ISBN: 9780312385873 (paperback).
In this fictionalized account of the man who may have betrayed Anne Frank, the author explores the historical context and the psychological needs of the man whose struggle to please his father and to provide for his family led to some of the horrors of World War II.

Marton, Kati. *Enemies of the People*, New York: Simon & Schuster, 2009, ISBN: 9781416586128.
Combining well-documented research and her own memories, Hungarian-American Kati Marton tells the true story of how her parents — freethinking journalists — endured the Nazi occupation of Budapest and imprisonment by the Russians during the Cold War. Interwoven in the story are Marton's recollections of the childhood trauma experienced by her and her sister.

Marton, Kati. *The Great Escape: Nine Jews Who Fled Hitler and Changed the World,* New York: Simon and Schuster, 2006,
ISBN: 9781615573523.
Marton chronicles the lives of nine Jewish men — four physicists, two filmmakers, two photographers and a writer — who made dangerous escapes from Hungary between the two world wars. Each one went on to make outstanding contributions that "changed the world" in their respective fields.

Ofer, Dahlia and Lenore J. Weitzman, eds. *Women in the Holocaust.* New Haven: Yale University Press, 1998, ISBN: 0300080808 (paperback).
This collection of personal narratives and scholarly essays reveals the courage and resourcefulness of women who endured and survived the hardships and vulnerabilities in the ghettos and concentration camps of the Holocaust.

Rosen, Iliana, ed. *Hungarian Jewish Women Survivors Remember the Holocaust: An Anthology of Life Histories,* Lanham, MD.: University Press of America, Inc., 2004, ISBN: 0761827048 (paperback).
Because many Hungarians believed that the Holocaust "can't happen here," some of the women whose stories are narrated in this anthology were shocked when the Nazis occupied Hungary. The stories — some written, some transcribed from oral interviews — reveal the personal courage and coping skills that the women displayed individually or, more often, with female relatives and friends as they conquered despair and survived the horrors of the Hungarian Holocaust.